# The Rushden Legacy

# —1—

ROGER, BARON RUSHDEN and holder of other lucrative honours, lieutenant in HRH's Own, was an extremely unhappy young man.

Those unaware of his family history might find this state ludicrous in one so graced with all the material advantages. But his lordship's forebears, while providing wealth, titles, and looks enough to satisfy any man, had also bequeathed a military tradition unbroken since the year 1193. Glorious service to sovereign and country was, for the males of the family, invariably accompanied by an early demise; not a one of them had survived past his thirtieth birthday.

The founder of the line had perished at age four-and-twenty while on Crusade with Richard Lion-Heart, and had been sent back to his small estates in a cedar coffin. Friends of this brave knight had thoughtfully provided for his sixteen-year-old widow and infant son by secreting the new-made baron's captured loot in a leather pouch within the coffin. Their aim was not strictly altruistic, as more than one of them had formed the intention of marrying the lady. They had reckoned, however, without the widow's determination to keep her late lord's property intact for their son, without the determination of the widow's vassals in protecting her, and without the cleverness, so atypical in a female of that time, that kept her suitors at each other's throats, making sure that one did not win what the others wanted. When she died, having led them all a merry dance for nearly twenty years, the young baron had attained his majority with his mother still unmarried and his inheritance still intact—though there had been considerable trouble in defence of both.

This second Rushden survived to the age of twenty-nine, but he, too, met his end on the field of battle and left a widow and young son. And so the pattern continued through the centuries. The Rushdens moved higher in the strata of Society, accrued more lands and wealth, and died military men. Some perished in wars, others in peacetime manoeuvers, and still others at sea on their way to or from arenas of conflict. And in an unbroken line stretching back to the last decade of the twelfth century, not one of them saw his thirtieth birthday.

Perhaps in compensation for this unfortunate history, however, the family also bequeathed to its sons physical characteristics that had tempted many generations of noble ladies to defy early widowhood for the attractions of marriage to a Rushden. The Rushdens never lacked for eligible females eager for their favours, which was one of the reasons for the family arrogance. Possession of a fine, pale complexion, golden hair, and blue eyes would have been enough, but when a Rushden male made his appearance, usually in uniform, hearts fluttered at the sight of the tall, elegant figure and proud-boned face, and the "curse" was forgotten. It need not be added that success on the battlefield was matched by success with the fair sex; let it suffice to say that one sixteenth-century holder of the title was found, upon his death, to have not less than twelve passionate love letters upon his person, all of them from titled women and none of them from his wife.

The present baron, twenty-eighth of that name, approached his thirtieth birthday with fatalistic trepidation. He was not married; he had no heir. He did, however, possess a multitude of sisters. If their husbands survived long enough, Rushden wives were great breeders. Roger's father, having produced, with his lady, a total of seven children (including a set of twins), succumbed just six weeks shy of his thirtieth birthday to the ministrations of his doctors after breaking three ribs, his collarbone, and an ankle during an encounter with a mettlesome Arab stallion. Thus had Roger succeeded to the title at the age of ten and to de jure rule over a houseful of women. That they adored and spoiled him was the blessing of his family situation, for when he assumed de facto authority at his majority he suddenly realised that his responsibilities included the dowering of his six sisters. Those worries, his duties in HRH's Own, the demands of the great estate of Midfield, and his whole-hearted devotion to the entirety of the female sex without single-hearted devotion to any one of its members, devoured his time. So at age nine-and-twenty years and two months, Roger, Baron Rushden, found himself a bachelor, likely to remain one, and a very unhappy young man indeed.

During March of 1808 there was very little for the dashing young officers stationed in London to do but ride, parade, be fitted for new uniforms, and dance attendance on the belles of the Season. These activities soon palled for some, and they turned to less socially acceptable means of combatting boredom while they waited for the next move that Bonaparte would make on the Continent. But though Society will tolerate a certain degree of rakehellishness in its bachelor members, it rarely forgives HRH's own extreme displeasure at not being invited to join the revels. And when the entertainment in question was given by the two most fashionable and decorated lieutenants in the Army, the royal pique was of epic proportions.

Lord Rushden and Michael, Viscount Hulme and the heir to an earldom, had not been engaged in anything so very different from the doings of their fellow officers. But their extravagance—and lack of sense—in choosing the most beautiful women, the most torrential flow of champagne, the most outrageous sums won and lost at the gaming tables, and the most elegant mansion in London as the site of their attempts to dispel Roger's gloom exceeded even their own previous exploits. As the Prince was returning from an irksome session at his father's palace he happened to pass Hulme House, noted the lights blazing at four in the morning, and quite naturally wondered what type of festivities were being held. Informed that the group "tearin' up old Cheltey's place" was headed by the earl's son, HRH presented himself at the door, certain of his welcome.

The footman who answered the door was no footman at all, but the young viscount himself. His arm was securely around the waist of a pretty countess who for eight months had resisted HRH's own blandishments but who obviously felt no constraint about combing her bejewelled fingers through the black curls covering his lordship's handsome head.

The subsequent discovery of three members of the royal family (obscure Continental connexions, to be sure) losing huge sums of money to Lord Rushden while Spanish gypsies plied the guests with champagne and guitar music completed HRH's fury. The next day Hulme House was closed down, the two young men were told to betake themselves to their estates, if their respective parents would have them, and their major was heard loudly bemoaning the evils of London.

"Well, we can't go to my place," Michael told his companion for the third time in as many hours. The brilliant sunshine of a March morning did nothing for his exquisitely throbbing eyes and skull, and only Roger's firm warning that if they stayed in London they would be drummed out of the regiment had persuaded Michael out of bed that morning. "My father, his eternal earlship, would have me drawn and quartered before I got past the gatekeeper's lodge at Chetley. And you, too," he added severely as a grin crossed Roger's face.

"Then we'll enjoy Midfield and my mother's tender mercies."

"That's the most insane idea you've had since you toasted Lady Hamilton in public! Damn it, Roger, slow down! I'm near death!"

Roger obligingly reined in his mount and regarded his suffering friend. "Really, Michael, Mama doesn't despise you as much as you think."

"Oh, doesn't she? And what about all those sisters of yours?" He shuddered, drawing the folds of his cloak closer as if to armour himself against Roger's siblings, the elder four of whom terrified him.

"Mary and Henrietta are safely involved in getting married—thank God. Elizabeth was visiting Yorkshire the last I heard, and I daresay Catherine and Caro are too much in awe of their new companion to cause any troubles at all. They've got a real dragon this time—Cathy wrote me only last week begging my help in ridding them of the formidable Miss Flitch. She says—"

"That is not who I meant and you know it," Michael said, colouring deeply.

"Oh, you refer to Anne?" Roger turned innocent eyes on his friend. "She may have a few brisk words for you, but—"

"If she speaks to me at all," Michael muttered.

"—But you can doubtless present your follies in this latest scrape as—"

"My follies? Who was it took two thousand from Herr Baron What's-his-name? Who insisted on hiring that damned troupe of gypsies? Who—" He stopped, not only recalling belatedly who had ordered so many cases of champagne but also remembering the black mood that had prompted the party in the first place. Roger had many years ago and after many brandies recited his dolourous family history. It had seemed silly to Michael at the time, but recently, as Roger approached his fatal birthday, it had taken all Michael's wits to distract him and keep him the carefree companion of their early youth. He sighed. "No hope for it. Good in you to keep me hidden from my father for a week or two—not to mention madame my stepmother." His face suddenly lit with irrepressible mischief. "I know! Let's go to Chetley first and tell him I've been banished for life!"

"To India," Roger agreed with a laugh. "But it's no use, Michael—he'd only believe you."

Midfield Hall was a day's hard ride from London and was, as its name suggested, situated in the midst of a wide grassy plain. Completed in the closing years of Elizabeth's reign, it had fine stained glass windows celebrating the six queens for whom Roger's six sisters had been named. The usual compliment of building in the shape of an *E* had been scorned by the succession of sixteenth-century barons who had erected the place on the site of their ancestral lands, but none of the builders had agreed on the precise design the house should take. Robert, the original planner, had wanted an *H*-shaped building, to honour the king who had added substantially to the Rushden wealth by dissolution of the monasteries, thus making Midfield possible. His son, John, had abbreviated the *H* into a graceless *U*. John's son Roger chose to return to his grandfather's original design, but had only just drawn up the plans when his own son William succeeded to the title. So Midfield

Hall followed an odd *J*-shaped plan, but since its hollow faced the river, anyone approaching the house saw only a symmetry of walls, windows, and chimneys on the long side of the building. In the previous century the house had almost become an architectural horror, for plans had been drawn to add a dome like the new one built at Castle Howard. Happily, gambling debts had commanded the share of the Rushden fortune that would have gone to this embellishment, and the long gallery and remains of the Great Hall remained intact without the ponderous addition the baron had planned.

But even without a dome there were oddities enough at Midfield, and not all of them were architectural. One might find cats in the drawing rooms; on the third floor of the family's wing there was a room that had once been a small aviary and that still breathed feathers when the windows were flung open. And guests were often astonished by the shrubbery maze that had no solution whatsoever. This had been the work of a particularly capricious baroness, who, after her lord's demise, had amused herself by altering the design until the whole planting was pointless. She had also started a rumour that a cache of crown plate was buried at the maze's centre, kept there for safety during the Civil Wars. Since the maze *had* no centre, she laughed herself silly every time she looked out her boudoir window to see her guests eagerly negotiating the tangles of shrubbery.

At Midfield as well could be found a fine collection of paintings and porcelains, and the tapestry in the long gallery had been worked by successive Ladies Rushden during their widowhoods. The most treasured of all the artworks, however, was a whimsical Lely depicting no fewer than five seventeenth-century baronesses, all widows, with the naked and squalling infant baron on his mother's lap.

Roger's mother had contributed only sparingly to the tapestry; her passion was gardens. This she had passed along to her daughters, and at any given season at least two of the young ladies could be found digging up plantings and organising new ones. Their love of the kitchens, however, was theirs alone, their mother deploring the habit that sent them at least once a week down to bake bread or cakes or pies with the servants. But even she had to admit that the results were excellent, and kept reasonable peace within a large and fractious family.

Roger adored his home and doted on his sisters, and regretted that his military career had left him so little time to pursue the life of a country gentleman. It was not that he did not enjoy carrying on the martial demands of the family tradition; indeed, it had afforded him great pride and pleasure. In the background these past months, however, there was always that sighing fatalism about his own demise. But his friend Michael had always been able to tell when he was feeling low, and could always laugh him out of it. Upon Roger's commission in the regiment he had encountered this only son of the Earl of Chetley, and their subsequent subtle competition in fashionable elegance had ended after an inconclusive fistfight in a back courtyard at Windsor. They had each then cheerfully forgotten all insults accrued and the actress over whom the fight had begun, and become fast friends. They were separated only when their duties to their families required brief sojourns at Midfield and Chetley Castle, respectively. And they visited often at each other's homes, although Michael had several excellent reasons for not frequenting Midfield as regularly as his friend stayed at Chetley.

Roger's mother deplored her son's unmarried state only slightly more than she detested his friend. Viscount Hulme might be the son of an earl and a fine matrimonial prize who at one time had seemed vastly pleased with her daughter Anne, but her ladyship could neither forget nor forgive the young man who had ridden into the courtyard at Midfield one morning yelling at the top of his lungs for Anne to present herself to him upon the instant. Anne had leaned out of her bedroom window, clad only in a thin lawn nightdress and the glory of her golden braids, and shrieked at him to go away and leave her in peace. Lady Rushden, listening and watching from behind the curtains of her own boudoir, had then been privileged to hear the viscount's exceedingly drunken proposal—not of marriage, but of elopement and an indecent establishment in London. Her most beautiful daughter had replied in phrases not generally associated with gently reared young ladies of quality. Anne had then slammed her windows shut, breaking three panes of seven-teenth-century glass in the process, and Michael had ridden away.

Lady Rushden never did learn how the indecent proposal had come about, nor why Anne had stayed in her room for two days afterward, refusing to show her face to anyone but her maid. When Roger had arrived that next evening with a bleary-eyed but cold sober Viscount Hulme in tow, her ladyship had declined to receive him. Roger had then taken her aside and smilingly given her the choice of receiving his friend or removing to her dower house.

That had been five years previous, but subsequent acquaintance-ship with Lord Hulme had not improved him in Lady Rushden's eyes. Anne usually managed to be on a protracted visit elsewhere when Roger arrived with his friend, and the very few times the two young people had met, the gentleman was very polite, the lady very cool. With the twin gadflies of a mother's concern and a devouring curiosity, Lady Rushden had once ventured to ask the cause of that early-morning descent on Midfield. Anne had stared and claimed not to recall the incident. Further questioning brought a more advanced case of amnesia. Lady Rushden decided to let well enough alone. As long as the viscount did not repeat his disgusting performance, she was willing to tolerate his presence in her house. Anything was preferable to her dower estate.

Yet, when her tall blond son and his dark-haired companion rode into the courtyard very late that March day, Lady Rushden permit-ted herself the luxury of one of her late lord's more colourful epithets before ringing violently for her butler.

"Calvert, serve my idiot son and his deplorable friend something to drink, and make sure their boots are clean before they walk on my carpets. I shall join them in the green drawing room in half an hour."

"Very good, my lady."

"And find Miss Anne. She should be with Miss Flitch, I think. Send her to me at once."

"Of course, my lady."

Calvert bowed and left the boudoir. Lady Rushden shut her *escritoire* with a snap, drumming her fingers atop its elegant inlaid surface. Five minutes later Anne appeared, a flour-coated apron around her waist and a scarf tied around her hair.

"You wished to see me, Mama?"

Her ladyship surveyed this prettiest and most accomplished of her six pretty and accomplished daughters. "I depend upon you to preside over supper tonight. I anticipate a headache."

The Honourable Anne Isabelle Louisa arched her delicate golden brows. "Have you had another letter from Henrietta about the wedding?" she asked sympathetically.

"No. Infinitely worse. Your brother is here with that wastrel friend of his. I did not summon him, since there is nothing here which requires his immediate attention, so I can only assume he is in some sort of trouble or other."

Anne nodded. "Thus the headache. I quite understand. I shall send Lily up to massage your neck for you after you've talked with Roger."

"You are a comfort to me, child. I shall miss you when you marry."

Anne hid a wince. Marriage was a sore subject with them, since at almost four-and-twenty she was not even betrothed. Her mother never missed an opportunity to remind her of the fact, though she had more or less given up her direct orders to find an eligible peer. "We'll meet them in the library, Mama?"

"The green room." Her ladyship glanced at the small gold clock on the table. "Another ten minutes, I think, for them to compose themselves—and for you to change your clothing."

"And for Roger to think up some plausible lie," Anne murmured.

"What was that, Anne?"

"Nothing, Mama. I'll come back directly I've washed."

Michael's discomfiture was not entirely due to the expected meeting with Miss Anne Rushden. He was badly in need of a strong drink, some food, and a change of clothes—particularly the latter, as Roger had insisted on their jumping their horses over every fence in Midfield park, with predictable effect on their attire. Michael was standing in front of the long mirror on the far side of the drawing room, trying to divest his coat and hair of local foliage, when Calvert's basso voice announced, "My lords, Lady Rushden and Miss Anne."

The baroness swept into the room, spared a disapproving glance for Michael, and went immediately to her son's side. Declining his affectionate kiss, she looked him straight in the eye and demanded, "What is it this time, Roger? Gambling, women, or drink?"

"All three, I'm afraid," he replied cheerfully. "Plus HRH himself. I've really done it this time, Mama; Michael and I both." He smiled at his sister. "In looks today, Annie. Keep Michael company while I regale Mother with the sordid details. Mama? The library for a moment, if you will indulge me."

"I have indulged you and your sisters for the past twenty-five years and more," she retorted as they walked through the connecting door to the library. "You say the Prince is involved? Good God, Roger, what have you done this time?"

The door closed on his answer, leaving Michael alone with Anne. He glanced at her apprehensively, then shrugged and decided to brazen it out. "Sorry to arrive so unexpectedly, Miss Rushden, but there was nothing for it but to leave town at once."

"So I gather." She seated herself decorously on a small sopha. "Oh, dear," she added as a muffled shriek issued from behind the library door. "I haven't heard Mama do that since she caught us swimming in the pond last summer. One would think Roger would be a touch more delicate with his bad news."

Michael shrugged again. "I'm more to blame then he, Miss Rushden." He paced to the windows, casting another anxious glance at the mirror as he did so, and picked a leaf from his curls. "It was my house, after all."

"Gambling, women, drink, and His Royal Highness," Anne mused. "Did you give a private entertainment and not invite him?"

"Worse," Michael said glumly. "He knocked on the front door."

She gave a choked little laugh. "Oh, truly, I don't know which of you is worse—you and Roger with your silliness, or the Prince with his crotchets." With a swish of muslin she was beside him. "Here," she said, laughter in her voice, "what an interesting ornament for a cravat!" She plucked at the article in question and held up a twig.

He was furious with himself for blushing. She calmly picked stray leaves from his coat, brushed off his back for him, and surveyed him at last with mocking eyes. "Better," she pronounced.

"Thank you, Miss Rushden," he said awkwardly.

She looked up at him, blue eyes filled with mirth, and suddenly they both began to laugh. He leaned back against the windowsill, grinning, about to tease her in return when a chilly voice broke their intimacy.

"I am relieved," Lady Rushden said quellingly, "though somewhat puzzled to find you taking this so hilariously. I see nothing amusing about my son's being packed off to the country in disgrace!"

Roger was behind her, looking rather sheepish. "I'm for a wash, Michael. You too, old man—you're a mess. Annie, be a darling and ring for Calvert. Tell him I left every stitch I own in London—so did Michael, for that matter—and we need comfortable clothes until our own arrive tomorrow. Mama, you'll excuse us until supper?" Without waiting for an answer, he gestured for Michael to follow him and they left the room, Michael pausing to direct a bow towards his hostess.

On the stairs leading to the family wing Roger whistled softly. "Lord! Thought she'd have an apoplexy! What were you and Annie laughing about?"

Michael grinned. "You know, I think she's finally forgiven me!"

"After five years? You're joking!"

"No, she actually talked to me. And smiled! It was just like the old days." He opened the door of his usual room and paused, a thoughtful expression on his face. "Not quite. She was a lovely little girl, but she's gotten quite beautiful."

Roger's eyes danced. "Have a care, Michael—don't want to have to call you out to defend my sister's honour!"

"You didn't the first time," Michael complained. They laughed again. "Besides, she doesn't need you to defend it, if it comes to that. Which it won't," he added hastily.

"I'm not sure but that I shouldn't pack you off to Chetley," Roger growled, the amusement in his eyes belying the tone of his voice. "Perhaps Lady Matilda and the Countess—"

"God, Roger, have mercy!"
Lord Rushden laughed again, clapped his friend on the shoulder, and retired to his own rooms.

# 2

IN LATE MARCH of 1808 a letter found its way from the marble corridors of one London mansion to the damasked library of another. Denuded of endless civilities, roundabout hints, and tactful evasions, the missive from Lord Fonteville to Lord Bellrose amounted to the following: You have an only daughter. I have an only son. Our lands adjoin. Why not combine the estates by combining the children in marriage?

It took some twenty minutes for the gist of this to penetrate Lord Bellrose's understanding. When it did, he rang for his butler, who sent for a footman, who located a maid, who informed Lady Diana that her parent desired her presence at once.

Diana set down her morning post and went directly to her father. Lord Bellrose waved his only child to a chair and stood for a moment squinting at her. Then, without further ado, he announced, "Fonteville and I have decided to marry you to Young George."

Diana turned all the colours of the rainbow. Springing to her feet and drawing herself to her full five feet six and one-half inches, she glared down at her father and demanded, "You have done what?"

"Time you got married, girl. Rising twenty-one, ain't you? Can't go round like this all your life. Young George is as good as any, and better than some." He paced restlessly away from her. "Sit down, Di. You put me in mind of your mother in a temper."

"Papa! This is absolutely out of the question!"

Lord Bellrose sat down, his small eyes narrowing as he contemplated the splendid sight of his daughter's outrage. Handsome filly, not a doubt of that, with her mother's tall figure and russet hair.

Hadn't her mother's curves, but breeding would fill her out. Ought to make fine children with Young George. He was tempted to voice the observation, but experience of her rages kept him silent on the subject.

What he did say was, "Young George will make you a fine husband. Land, title, honours, money—good family, fine house at Siddensley—" Lord Bellrose fidgeted. "Look here, Di, it's more than time you were married! Been half a score young bucks in here this last twelvemonth, begging me to use my influence to get you to marry 'em!"

"Surely not all of them at once, Papa! There are laws against polyandry."

"None of your impertinence!" Lord Bellrose was not certain what "polyandry" meant, but there was no mistaking Diana's tone. "You're to marry Young George and there's an end to it." At the sudden sparkle of tears in her eyes, his voice softened. "There, child, Young George is a fine figure of a man. He'll be a good husband to you and give you lots of pretty little boys and girls. You'll be very happy."

Diana's tears were caused by utter frustration. It was not that she was in love with someone else—she played the game far too well and with too much enthusiasm to allow herself to fall in love with any of her suitors—but she suddenly realised that by keeping herself free of even a hinted attachment she had left the way clear for this disaster. The prospect of being buried in the country at Siddensley with Young George, a hundred boring neighbours, and endless children to ruin her figure made the tears flow in earnest. "I won't!"

Her father spluttered, then roared, "By God, missie, you will! Go to your rooms and prepare to receive your future husband tonight at dinner!"

Recognising the mulish expression before which even a prime minister had quailed, Diana took refuge in flight to her rooms and a passion of tears.

Two hours and much reflexion later, mostly on the horrors of being married to Young George, Diana realised that her only hope lay in making herself so disagreeable that the gentleman would rather join Bonaparte's army than marry her. She had encountered Young George several times and retained no very kind memories of him. He had danced with her at Lady Frewe's, tramped on her feet, and spent most of the evening dogging the steps of Miss Kitty Kirby. Diana sniffed; that pink-and-white simpering miss was just Young George's type. All Diana would have to do would be to present herself as the precise opposite of that witless sugarplum, and Young George would be so revolted that he would refuse even to contemplate the marriage.

Her spirits sank momentarily at the idea of anyone, much less Young George, thwarting formidable Old George in anything. But she rallied when she reminded herself that she would be showing Fonteville *père* just how unsuitable a wife she would make for his son. She would be haughty, opinionated, and stubborn; no man in his right mind would wish to saddle himself with such a bride.

Lady Diana rose from her bed and rang for her maid. Part of the evening's campaign required daring clothes, since Kitty Kirby's dresses were the height of fashion for twelve-year-olds. As Diana handed an emerald silk to Betsy for mending, she reflected with satisfaction that Young George certainly would not want a wife with such shocking—and shockingly expensive—taste in dresses.

Then she sighed. Reluctant as she was to admit it, her father had been right about one thing. It was time she found a husband. She had had a lovely time enjoying the attentions of the city's most handsome and interesting young men; she adored the excitement of being a reigning belle; but she also knew that one could not go on like that forever. She was, as her father had so tactlessly pointed out, approaching her twenty-first birthday. Another year or so and she would be looked on as a hopeless old spinster.

Lady Diana consoled herself with a solitary tea and the penning of a long letter to her dearest friend, Miss Anne Rushden. Anne was the only young lady of Diana's acquaintance who could be trusted to sympathise with her predicament, appreciate her scheme regarding Young George, and commiserate with her on the unfairness of marriage.

Young George—or, to give him his due, George William Henry

Algernon, Viscount Trouse—sat across the table from his intended bride, watching her with quick glances of his close-set brown eyes. His encounters with the fair sex had not been, by and large, resounding successes. But although his understanding was not keen and he was more inclined to silence than conversation in the presence of a pretty, fashionable female, he did understand that whatever interest they accorded him was due more to his name and fortune than to his person. Young George was a generous young man, however, and attributed this to the young ladies' mamas, who had trained them from birth in the arts that would capture wealth without paying too much attention to wit. In many ways he was, in fact, indebted to this mercenary turn of female mind, for it assured him that degree of notice that title and fortune must always attract. His vanity, therefore, was pleased; he fed it regularly on the delighted smiles of dowagers when he danced with their plain daughters, on the frequent mental enumeration of his acres and his shares, and on the certainty that his reputation as a gentleman was spotless. He did not gamble, drank only port and champagne, took no interest in racing, did not involve himself in the undignified prattle of politics, had no friends who were whispered about, never did anything out of the ordinary or spoke a word that was not labouriously preconsidered. He was, in short, the type of well-bred British bore that was everything Diana loathed.

She was at her most dazzling. In the hour before dinner she had attempted to engage him in an argument about politics, in which he had, of course, not the slightest interest. On their way in to dinner she had enquired his opinion on the situation in the Peninsula, which only made him shrug. At table she leaned across her plate, giving him an ample view of creamy shoulders and décolletage, and aired her views on the current state of the poetical arts. In between pronouncements she ate heartily of the lamb with a most unladylike appetite and called twice for her wineglass to be refilled. Young George said nothing.

Lady Diana, not knowing if he was either so disgusted as to be incapable of conversation or so lackwit as to be incapable of holding an opinion on anything, dug into her dessert with a will. She adored lemon mousse but tasted little of it, intent instead on making herself out to be the exact antithesis of timid, nibbling Kitty Kirby. She was fully aware of Young George's covert peeks at her and despite herself was somewhat embarrassed at the depth of her neckline. It was a wretched meal, designed to give even the strongest constitution an attack of indigestion, and thus when her father signalled to her that she might excuse herself, she fled eagerly so that the men could have their port and cigars and she could have a little peace. She paced about the drawing room, chewing her lip. She wished Anne Rushden present to buoy her spirits with a conspiratorial grin; she wished she suddenly did not feel so certain of failure; she wished Young George to the Antipodes. When the drawing room doors parted to reveal her father, Lord Fonteville, and Young George, she nearly jumped.

"Diana," Lord Bellrose said with high good humour and a significant glance at Lord Fonteville, "why don't you show this young man the new flowerbeds we've put in? Hayes lit the outside torches, so you'll have some light."

Diana tried not to gulp. She favored Young George with a wide smile. He bowed gravely and extended his arm. Taking it, she asked, "Do you take an interest in flowers, my lord?"

"Not in their cultivation," he replied solemnly, and conducted her out onto the terrace and thence to the pathway that wound through the fine gardens behind the house.

By the flickering light of the torches the vista was romantic and beautiful. Trees and hedges took on magical shapes, and the scent of new herbs bordering the flowerbeds was intoxicating in the moonlight—or would have been so with almost any other companion than Young George. Diana cast about for something to say, could think of nothing, and was about to turn in desperation to something trite about the weather when Young George spoke.

"Let me be plain, Lady Diana."

She stopped walking, picked a twig off a rosebush, and began to shred it. "Pray, do."

Young George pulled in a deep breath and exhaled a strong aroma of port. He had obviously fortified himself well for his speech. "Our parents wish us to make a match. I cannot say I have formed any deep attachment for you, but I am sure this will come in time. It is in every way suitable and proper that we should be wed. Our families are equal, and that is important, but what is even more essential is that we are naturally inclined towards each other by reason of our inheritances. What could be more fitting than that our two estates should be joined by our marriage? It is this natural affinity which—''

''Oh, really!'' She tore the leaves off the twig with short, sharp motions, having heard quite enough insults. ''There is no affinity between us at all, my lord. We do not share the same views, we are wholly opposed in character—''

''A wife must hold her husband's views, and as to your character, I am sure that marriage can only alter it for the better.''

She gasped in outrage. ''Hold her husband's views—! Alter my character—! My lord, you are pleased to insult me!''

Unruffled, he took the shredded stick from her hands and tossed it into the flowerbeds, retaining one of her hands in the process. ''As my wife, you will of course defer to my opinions.''

''And have you any?'' she snapped. ''You have no politics that I can tell, no interest in the issues of our day, the literature, music, ideas—even the flowers! And now you say that your wife will hold your views!'' She glared at him. ''Is your bride to be a mindless mimic? If so, you had best give her something *to* mimic!''

''Lower your voice. You are shouting.''

''I will shout if I please. I am not going to marry you, my lord!''

''You will marry me, Lady Diana, because our fathers wish it. And so do I.''

''I will not!'' She turned to go, tugging her hand free of his grasp, then whirled again. ''You see how charmingly we would deal with each other? You bring out the shrew in me, and no doubt I disgust you—indeed, you have said as much with your implication that my character will change for the better!'' She tried more quietly. ''We would be miserable, my lord. Do give it up. You don't really wish to marry me.''

''I do, and I shall,'' he replied stubbornly.

''In the name of God, why?'' she exploded.

''Because it is appropriate and fitting that our lands and blood be joined—''

"Oh, rubbish! I would make you an even worse wife than you would make me a husband! Come, George, reflect for a moment on what it would be like. You would have a wife with strong opinions who is not afraid of airing them. I have expensive tastes in clothes and jewels, and would be in town more than half the year attending parties and the Opera—"

"Those things will change, as I have said."

His obstinacy began to frighten her. She had dealt with that quality in her father, and the prospect of a husband with the same failing horrified her. Desperately she cast about for something to convince him that she was no fitting bride for him. What could she possibly say that would make him go away and leave her in peace?

"I am already committed in another direction!" she blurted.

For the first time he wavered. "You are—to whom? How far goes this commitment?"

"Marriage!" Diana gasped. "I am secretly engaged to be married, my lord. I did not speak of it before because my father does not know!" Pausing for breath and inspiration, she tried to calm herself as she sent her mind searching for a likely or even an unlikely name, hoping all the while that she would not be forced to give one.

"Of what duration is this engagement?" Young George's heavy brows were drawn together into a single line over his nose.

"Oh, a long time." She trusted that the twisting of her hands would be taken for fear of discovery rather than fear of being caught in such a lie. "If my father found out—"

"He must find out sooner or later. Who is the man? I have a right to know."

"I cannot, really I cannot—" She bit her lips, thinking frantically.

"I will not inform your father, Lady Diana," Young George said with awful dignity. "Your guilty secret is your own shame to bear."

"I am ashamed," she whispered, breathing a little more easily now. Surely he would press her no more for the name. A good thing, too, for her mind was a total blank. "I am so sorry, George. It is wicked in me to keep it from my father, but especially to allow you to hope. I had thought that to persuade you of the impossible differences between us might alter your opinion of our marriage." Her tongue moved more easily as she warmed to her topic. "But you were so overwhelming that I simply could not keep my secret from you any longer. And indeed you deserve to know about the engagement, so that you will not think you appear in a bad light in my father's eyes, or indeed, in my own—you were simply masterful, so . . ." She trailed off helplessly, stealing a glance at him from beneath her lashes. Flattery never hurt, she reflected as he took on a puffed-up air at what he had presumed was a compliment. But in the next instant her satisfaction shattered.

"His name, Lady Diana."

Diana opened her mouth, closed it, and gave a little squeak of dismay. Who on earth could she name? Panic whipped at her brain; her lips parted, and she cried out, "Lord Rushden!" not knowing whence the name had appeared in her mind or on her lips. "He is the brother of my dear friend Miss Anne Rushden, and he and I—"

Young George's shoulders stiffened. "An unsuitable but understandable match. Lord Rushden is easily the most dissolute wastrel in his regiment—with the possible exception of his companion, Lord Hulme. I quite understand your reluctance to mention his name to your father, especially since their most recent disgrace."

She blinked, trying to recall the incident, then remembered something said a fortnight ago about HRH and an all-night revel at Hulme House. The ensuing scandal had been supplanted by a shocking elopement and a fortune lost at cards, but she decided instantly to use the by-now-forgotten gossip for all it was worth. She thanked God that Lord Rushden had dissolute habits.

"Please," she murmured, making a creditable job of it, "do not torment me so. I know his faults, but can a woman ever help herself when her heart is lost?" She sneaked another look at him and nearly giggled. Young George's expression was a miracle of pomposity, and his eyes had almost disappeared under his heavy brows. She had to turn away from him to hide her grin, for the thought had also just struck her that she had no idea what Lord Rushden looked like, other than that he had blond hair. And what was his first name, anyway? Robert? Something like that. A little cough of laughter escaped her and she clapped her hand over her mouth.

"Be assured, Lady Diana, that I will say nothing of this to your father or to mine. It will remain your guilty secret." He seemed to relish the phrase, for he repeated it as he passed his handkerchief over her shoulder. "I shall merely say that upon closer conversation I realised that a life with you would be insupportable for a variety of reasons."

She turned to give him a tearful smile of gratitude, handing back the scrap of lace. "You are too kind, George," she said in a dulcet tone.

"It is more than you deserve," he acknowledged, obviously enjoying his role of rejected lover, even more so because he could feel himself so vastly superior to the other gentleman in question. Diana realised that she could have chosen no one in England more calculated to satisfy Young George's conceit. "Are you ready to return to the house? We should inform our parents without delay."

She quivered at the thought of Old George's fury, not to mention her own father's, but rallied and took his arm. "Thank you, my lord. I appreciate your compassion. And I sincerely believe you will find a lady more worthy of you than I."

He missed the sarcasm and merely nodded. Escorting her back into the drawing room, they came upon the two peers sitting over a game of cards. Lord Bellrose looked up first and, taking his daughter's moist eyes as ample justification of his hopes, glowed with pleased pride. Then he looked at Young George, whose face was not at all what he would have expected from the successful suitor of so fine a prize as his daughter. Lord Bellrose's expression clouded and then collapsed into a mixture of anger, bewilderment, and suspicion.

"I regret to inform your lordships," Young George said, taking Diana's hand ostentatiously from his arm, "that circumstances make it impossible for us to wed."

Old George's white head swivelled round, his eyes blazing. "What's this? What's this?" he barked. "Not get married?"

Before anyone could say anything else, Diana made her curtsey and said breathlessly, "Pray excuse me—I cannot bear—good night!"

Safe in her boudoir upstairs, she indulged in the blessed relief of laughter. Her face buried in a pillow, she giggled until her sides ached. Free, she repeated to herself; there would be no marriage to odious Young George!

The front door slammed with a shudder that reverberated through the whole house, and Diana laughed again as she reminded herself to have Hayes send for a joiner in the morning for the hinges. By the time she finally regained her composure it was time for Betsy to help her undress and braid her hair for the night. Diana kept her colour and her mirth in check—she was not one of those ladies who share thoughts and feelings with their servants—then dismissed Betsy and threw herself back on her bed, smiling.

Dearest Anne, to have such a convenient brother! Diana went to her writing desk to begin another letter to Anne detailing the night's events. Her friend could be trusted to keep the jest to herself and to laugh over it just as hard as Diana had done. Gleefully Diana wrote,

> *My Dear Annie,*
> *I hope you do not mind, but I borrowed your Brother for ten minutes tonight. Such a famous Scheme, even better than the tricks we played on tedious Lady Dandridge at Bath together last year, do you remember? My first Plan, which I outlined in my last letter, met with only slight Success, so I did a most shameless thing which shames me not at all! I am the most Horrid Female in the world, but I have confidence that my Dear Annie will enjoy the tale as much as I did in telling it to Young George.*

For another hour her pen flew, painting an extravagant and hilariously funny portrait of herself and Young George, and she retired at last to her bed with a catlike smile of satisfaction on her face.

# 3

"ROGER, I BEG you will be serious!"

"I assure you, Mama, I am in deadly earnest."

Lady Rushden cast a baleful glare upon her son. "You never look it," she reproved. "In all the days you have been home I have never once seen you without a smile on your lips."

"What face I have is what you and Papa gave me," he said with a grin. "It cannot, alas, be exchanged. And besides, Mama, I am happy here." He strolled to the window of the morning room and looked out across the lawns to the river. "I had forgotten how beautiful Midfield is."

"Roger," his mother said severely, "we must decide what to do about your disgrace. I have heard from Letitia and your Aunt Sturbrough, and along with others they are of the same opinion. Your riotous mode of life must come to an end. The only way to reestablish your credit in Society and ease the Prince's distaste will be to conform to standards."

"You would condemn me to ceaseless boredom, Mother. And I do not see what effect an alteration in my style of life would have on HRH, who is not exactly sedate in his own manner of entertaining himself."

"I tell you to your head, young man, it is time you settled! You have a position to uphold and duties to an old and honourable name." Her ladyship set down her coffee cup with a rattle of china. "Have you ever seen the inside of the House? I thought not! The Rushdens have always been a political family, and—"

"Oh, come, Mama," Roger said, turning to smile at her. "Grandfather only showed his face there when it was impossible to avoid it, and as for Father—the closest he ever came to active service in Parliament was when he entered its halls to challenge Cousin Richard to a duel! Over yourself, before you were married to him, if I recall the scandal correctly.''

Her ladyship had the grace to blush. ''Nonsense. Your father and grandfather might not have taken their seats with any regularity, but they always were part of the power—''

''With all our land and money—and our interests in foreign trade—it would be quite unnatural if the government did not consult the Rushdens. It could scarcely have done without Great-grandfather's inestimable advice on how not to avoid financial ruin. He was familiar enough with that condition, God knows!''

''Roger, your want of respect sets a deplorable example for your sisters,'' Lady Rushden chided, wisely refraining from comment on her son's last and, unhappily, true statement. ''Which is another reason I insist on modification of your present mode of life. Heaven knows I was hard put to see Mary and Henrietta properly settled, with such a rakehell of a brother to prejudice their interests in Society.''

''Now, that is hardly fair!'' Stung, Roger began to pace. ''Hetty's been promised to John forever, and as for Mary, if any man could not instantly adore the sweetest and most beautiful—''

''I am not talking of their matches,'' his mother said forbiddingly. ''But of the whispers behind their backs. Whispers about you, sir! Your entertainment, your friends, your gambling—''

''At least I win—not like Great-grandfather!''

''—your mistresses!''

''Madame, you are very close to exposing the worst side of my temper,'' he warned. ''Need I remind you that as head of this family, I can pack you out of this house without a by-your-leave?''

''Don't be absurd, Roger!'' she countered. ''You have four other sisters who must needs find husbands. Anne has been out for four years, and not one offer has been made for her. As for Elizabeth—'' She shrugged. ''Once she gets over her ridiculous *tendre* for Lord Gerald, I have wonderful hopes of a match with Lord Dewberry's son. But what of Caroline and Catherine? They will come out this year at last, since their elder sisters are to be married—also at last!—

and there shall still be four to settle!" She rose majestically to her feet, eyes snapping. "Have you no concern for the credit of your sisters?"

"I have the greatest concern for them. I love them all." Roger tore at the fringe of a bell pull, ripping it slowly to shreds. "I would never do anything that would damage—"

"Then why do you persist in these reprehensible—"

He faced her, his expression hard. "I will shortly turn thirty, Mama—or at least, my thirtieth birthday approaches. Considering the history of our family, I do not think you shall have to worry about my conduct for more than another few months."

"Roger!" Thunderstruck, her ladyship collapsed back onto the sopha with her hand at her throat. "Never say such things!"

"Why not? We all know it to be true." He strode to the door, the heels of his riding boots digging deeply into her carpets. "So I will obey your wishes, Mama, and adhere to your tender sentiments— and I will even, dearest Mama, find myself a wife and marry before the end of the spring. For though I am most sensible of the points you have mentioned about my sisters, I have also not the slightest wish to be the last of my line. With some luck, you should be greeting the twenty-ninth baron about four months after I am dead." He turned, sketched a bow in her direction, and finished, "I have an appointment with Anne to go riding. Your servant, my lady."

At the stables Roger was greeted by the head groom with the intelligence that "Missie Anne h'a gune tearin' oot li' a bullet fired, m'laird." With a disapproving shake of his head the old man continued. "Missie Anne will nae be wantin' company, m'laird, but i' me t'were thee, t'would be settin' oot after young missie, t'would."

"Thank you, MacTaggart. Which direction did she take?" He checked the girth on his favourite mount and vaulted lightly into the saddle.

"Past yon gate, oot ontae the doons, m'laird. 'Tis mortal furied she were, aye."

"I'll find her. I presume she took Daystar?"

MacTaggart shook his head. "Nay, m'laird, she moonted on the blooded de'il o' t'other young laird's.''

Roger saw red. "You allowed my sister to ride out of here on Lord Hulme's stallion?'' he roared.

" 'Twas nae to young missie, m'laird. Ye ken the temper o' this clan!''

"Indeed I do,'' he snapped, and spurred his horse toward the east gate. Michael's fire-eating Zenith was restive on the best of days, and certainly no fit mount for a young lady, even if that young lady had been riding almost every day of her life since the age of five. Jumping hedges and streamlets, he counted the days since he and Michael had exercised their horses and was appalled to find that the stallions had not been out for eight days. He finally reached the downs and galloped across them at high speed, his worry for his sister increasing with every beat of Saladin's powerful hooves.

At last he caught sight of her, and with something of a feeling of anticlimax, for the huge horse was walking most calmly along the edge of a wood. Roger slowed his stallion, called out a greeting in a voice usually reserved for the parade ground, and Anne turned to wave at him. When he caught up to her, recovering his breath after the wild ride, he noted that although she was flushed, she was a good deal more composed than MacTaggart had led him to believe.

"What d'you think you're doing, stealing Michael's horse?''

"Don't be so gothick, Roger,'' she retorted, swinging the stallion around to ride beside him. "I can ride anything ever shod, and you know it. And since your friend has not seen fit to exercise his horse anytime this past week, I thought to do him a favour.'' She patted Zenith's high-arched neck. "We've had a regular gallop, haven't we, old man?''

"Don't put me off with that, Annie,'' Roger said severely. "Mac-Taggart said you tore out of the stables in a rage. I want to know why.''

She glanced at him, blue eyes kindling. "I do not recall having given you leave to act as my substitute father. You may be the head of the family and I nothing but a sister, but I can think of instances still when I saved your miserable skin for you when Mama was ready to murder you.''

"Annie,'' he said in a softer tone, "what's wrong?''

She sighed quietly. They rode for a time in silence, and as he looked at her he realised that Michael's assessment had been correct: Anne had been a lovely girl, but she had grown into a most beautiful woman. A man rarely takes notice of a sister's looks until she can do him credit in Society or until those looks are commented upon by other men. Roger was pleased to find that Anne, though not as tall as Henrietta or Elizabeth, was more finely made and sunnily blond than either of those two pretty young ladies. Anne's pure gold hair was pulled severely back from her face and mostly hidden by her hat and veil, but the escaping tendrils curled round her cheeks and neck most charmingly. Her nose, though long like all the family's, was delicately moulded, her large eyes were set wide in her oval face, and her bearing was graceful and assured. He felt a rush of satisfaction; she was a sister to be proud of.

"I doubt you could understand the problem," Anne said after a few minutes.

"Is it Michael? Do you want me to send him home to his father?"

She gave him a sharp look, than laughed. "Oh, heavens no! You could not be so cruel as to pack him off to the terrifying earl!"

"Answer me, Annie."

"Very well," she said reluctantly. "It is Lord Hulme—partly. Roger, why does he behave so oddly to me? I have given him every reassurance that we can be friends again, but it appears he is not so inclined."

Roger chuckled. "Don't you see it? Michael has been insanely in love with you this age! I very much doubt he wishes to be your *friend,* love."

"Roger!" Anne blushed poppy pink. "How dare you tease me!"

"It isn't teasing, love, it's the truth. And I forbid you to tell Michael I have given away his secret. I don't think he realises it himself."

"Oh, of course he is in love with me," she scoffed. "A man wild in love with one lady must naturally spend his time with others— most of them of doubtful reputation—and not excluding the highborn ones who act like the commonest whores!"

"Such language!" He grinned. "A man must amuse himself, after all. And you must admit you've given poor Michael no encourage-

27

ment. Cold as an icicle, never more than polite to him, rarely here when I bring him—poor lad, it's a wonder he has his sanity."

"Sanity? I beg to agree with Mama. Neither of you is the slightest bit sane. Well, we shall see about Michael, I suppose."

"And after that little stunt of five years ago—you never did tell me the whole of that, and Michael is mute on the subject."

"That is my business. But I have some news for you, Roger. It concerns the Lady Diana Bellrose."

"Who?"

"Diana Bellrose. Surely you recall her," she insisted. "She was here not two summers ago, visiting me."

Roger frowned, thinking. Then he nodded. "Ah, yes . . . tall girl, redheaded, thin, nothing to recommend her but her eyes—and her affection for you, of course," he added hastily.

"Wretch! She is certainly tall, with reddish hair, but she has improved in other ways, I assure you."

"I am sorry, but I do not remember her in town. Perhaps we move in different circles." He winked.

"I certainly hope that you do! Anyway, I am glad that you remember her, for I scarcely know how to begin the tale."

"You have succeeded in diverting me from the subject of yourself and Michael," he said and grinned at her. "Pray go on."

"Well, you see, she has been ordered by her father to marry a man she despises."

"What does that signify? Who in the world is allowed to marry for love?"

Anne turned wide eyes on him. "Roger! How bitter you sound!"

He shrugged and smiled at her, but he could not keep his sudden depression from his face or voice. "Mama is at me to settle again, you know, and it would appear that settling includes marriage. Although she did not say as much, I know that is in her mind. I am not averse to it—I must provide an heir, you see, and I have only a few months in which to do it. I must marry, and soon, and get my wife with child, and—"

"Roger!" Anne reined in her horse and reached over to shake his arm. "That is all nonsense! I pray you will not be so idiotish! There is no earthly reason why you should not live to be ninety.''

"No reason except that of the twenty-seven previous Lords Rushden, not one of them has seen his thirtieth birthday. So, I must find some girl and get married.''

"And have you decided which lady you will honour?'' she asked tartly.

"If I had the slightest notion, I would be on my knees proposing at this minute. The horror of it is, I do not know one single woman with whom it would not be a burden to spend a week's time, let alone the last month's of one's life.''

"Do not be so morbid!''

"I am attempting to be realistic—for the first time in my life.'' He shrugged. "No escaping it, Annie. It is mid-March; my birthday is in January. I have lived with no thought to anything by my own amusement, this I freely admit, but this year I have come to realise that I no longer have a choice.''

"Roger . . . I could not bear it for you to marry without love.''

"Ah, but would it be good in me to marry a lady I could love, when our time together must necessarily be so brief?'' He shook his head. "I have always thought—when I bothered to think at all— that I should simply remain unwed and let one of you girls provide a male heir. He could take the Rushden name and title, and the line would be preserved without my having made any widows.''

"It is nothing but superstition!'' she cried. "The Rushdens probably got themselves killed a-purpose to give everyone else something to talk about!''

He laughed briefly. "It's all right, Annie; I don't really mind. Don't distress yourself so. I should like to see the twenty-ninth baron, but if I do not, I'm sure one of you girls will have a little boy to take over the name. Still I owe it to Mama to try.''

"I forbid you to say anything more on the subject!'' Anne stated firmly, but with tears in her lovely eyes. "Or, if you feel you must, talk about it with Michael. For all his faults, he has a good heart and is steadier than people believe him to be. He will convince you that all this is nonsense. You'll be able to find a lady to love and esteem, and you'll marry and live to a colossal age.''

"I see you have made a study of Michael's character," he noted. She coloured. "If you intend to be rude, I shall return to the house."

"No, forgive me, Annie . . . I should not tease you. I will talk with Michael if you wish, but he knows all about this and not even he can convince me otherwise on the subject. I shall marry someone, and soon, and hope I can get her with child before the inevitable."

"What a cold fish you can be, Roger!"

"Nay, love, only practical. And it is all only a hum at this point, anyway. Now tell me all about your unfortunate friend, Lady Diana Bellamy."

"Bellrose," she corrected, "and I'll wager you'll have good reason to remember the name in time!"

With that she dug her heels into Zenith's ribs and the stallion was off like a pistol shot across the downs. Roger swore, laughed, and set off after her, intending to demand her meaning. But by the time he caught up with the fleet Zenith, they were at the front drive. Their mother and two younger sisters, in company with the whey-faced Miss Flitch, were setting off in the carriage to visit neighbours. Anne offered to ride along, and they departed, leaving Roger alone and thoughtful.

# === 4 ===

LADY DIANA HAD adequately impressed upon her father the necessity of attending Lady Frewe's ball two nights after the debacle with the Georges. Lord Bellrose was originally of the opinion that she should stay home out of maidenly modesty and, incidentally, to explain fully to him why she and Young George had not gotten on. Diana had used tactics of which Bonaparte might have approved in avoiding all explanations with her father until the day of the ball. But that morning she finally stamped her foot in its blue kid slipper and declared she would not sit home and be gossiped about for something that was not her fault. Could she help it, she cried, if Young George had found her physically repugnant?

Since his daughter was the image of his late wife, Lord Bellrose's anger turned quite effectively to Young George. They went to the ball that evening, Diana in pale peach silk and her mother's diamonds, which his lordship had given her by way of compensating for the loss of Young George. It was now his view that the fool had no sense at all and he intended to make the view known at Lady Frewe's.

He escorted his radiant daughter through the receiving line, bowing and chatting, not understanding the arch looks given them by various of their acquaintance. But even he could not fail to note the meaning of Lady Frewe's greeting to them, which gave him a shock that left him speechless and nearly insensible with astonishment. This state was nothing compared to the extremity of Lady Diana's agitation when Lady Frewe beamed on her with a kittenish smile and exclamations of surprise.

"Why, here is the minx now! Diana, dearest creature, I am

undone! But of course, we all are! You and Lord Rushden! How ever did you manage to attach him?''

Diana turned white, then fiery red, and stammered, ''I—I'm sure I don't—''

Lady Frewe tweaked her chin with sharp nails. ''Minx!'' she repeated. ''All this time you've kept so many of our young men dangling after you, while you were secretly engaged to darling Roger! A miraculous catch, dearest creature!''

Diana's green eyes narrowed with suspicion and then widened with certainty. Damn Young George, she thought furiously. She managed a smile, bent her head as if embarrassed rather than utterly humiliated, and murmured, ''I hardly know what to say, Lady Frewe. Your sources of information—''

''Are impeccable, since I had it from Sylvie Kilgore, who heard it direct from Lord Fonteville. When is the happy day?''

''I cannot tell at present, my lady.'' The happiest of days for her would be when she found Young George and drew blood.

''Well, you have sunk all your suitors into hopelessness. Adam Pendale is talking of a duel with Roger—and of course Charles Pryce has simply gone off to the country in despair.''

''I trust the wholesome air of Yorkshire will cure him in all haste,'' Diana said, then gave a pretty start of surprise. ''Oh, pray excuse us, Lady Frewe, I simply must speak with Miss Kirby.'' She flashed a wide smile and, taking her father's arm in a grip more suited to a mettlesome horse than her parent, steered him toward the windows. She had of course no idea where Miss Kirby was and did not care; she only knew she had somehow to explain to her father, who had turned six shades of crimson in as many minutes and seemed dangerously close to recovering his powers of speech.

She was correct. ''Now, miss!'' he exploded. ''What's all this? Engaged to Rushden? When did this happen?''

''Please, Papa,'' she begged, casting nervous eyes around the assembly, mortified lest anyone overhear. ''Only listen for a moment—''

''How did this come about? First I've heard of it! Why didn't you tell me?''

''Papa,'' she pleaded once more, urging him to an alcove and seating them both on a small bench where a potted palm tree screened them from view. "Only give me time to explain—"

"Not that he isn't a fine match for you," Lord Bellrose continued with a sudden smile. He was mercifully silent for a time. Then he grinned widely and slapped his own thigh. "By God, Di, you're a contrary baggage! Playing with all those young bucks while engaged to another man! I wager he don't much like you chasin' around to parties without him, eh? You'll make him a fine Lady Rushden, I daresay. What a secret to hold from your father! Rushden!"

She sighed deeply, resigned to her fate. "I am truly sorry, Papa, but . . ." She trailed off helplessly, trying once again to recall what the man looked like. She had seen him, she was sure, but could not for the life of her remember his features. And what had Lady Frewe said his first name was? Roger?

Lord Bellrose took her loss of words for shyness—odd since she had never had a shy day in her life, but he subscribed to the theory of feminine behaviour rather than its actuality. "There, Di," he said with a chuckle, "I won't quiz you. It's time we joined everyone else and you received your congratulations. When d'you expect Rushden in town? I'll give you a big party, invite everyone who's anyone, to formally announce the engagement."

The concept staggered her, but she gathered her wits enough to plead, "Papa, pray do not let us forget Lord Rushden's hand in this! After he informs his mother and sisters—and gives his permission for the announcement to be made—" Impossible. This entire conversation was a nightmarish impossibility, but far worse to contemplate what would happen to her when Lord Rushden heard about it.

"So you're to be ruled by him in this, eh?" He glanced at her shrewdly. "Must say ruling you won't be easy. I've tried for years and I don't envy him. But he's getting a fine filly and I trust he knows it. Looks, breeding, money, family connexions, position— I'll have my man of business talk with his about the contracts as soon as may be." He patted her hand and helped her to her feet. "There, Di, all's forgiven. I'm mightily pleased, I don't mind saying so. What a wedding it will be, eh?"

She smiled weakly, thinking it would be a fine event indeed—but for the absence of the bridegroom, it would have been the wedding of the year. "Yes, Papa. May we go directly to the refreshment table? I fear I'm quite thirsty."

"Splendid idea. Need some champagne myself. Come along, Di."

During the next four hours Lady Diana dosed herself liberally with champagne. She needed it. Except for three dances, all of them with older gentlemen of her father's acquaintance, she had occupied a chair next to the prosy old Dowager Countess of Chekewode, who was growing a bit forgetful in her old age and expressed fresh congratulations to Diana every time she looked at her. Wallflower! She picked at a loose thread on a China silk fan, folded it, unfolded it again to look at the delicate butterflies captured on the fine panel.

"And so sly, dearest Diana," Lady Chekewode said for the dozenth time, tittering.

She turned to smile, and longed for escape. A footman passing with a tray of champagne gave her the excuse she needed, and she took her leave of the countess after promising to return directly. Snatching a glass from the tray, she drained it swiftly and took another. Her feet tapped irresistibly to the music from the string orchestra. She wanted to dance—and not with one of her father's clumsy friends. She wanted to glide across the floor clasped in the arms of a young and handsome gentleman—that had been her part since she had first come out into Society, and its sudden and humiliating end was something she resented with all her heart. Damn Young George! she thought angrily and, turning to set the second emptied glass down, found herself face to chagrined face with the gentleman in question.

"Good evening, my lord!" she cried. "I have been looking for you this age! And here in happy hour, I find you at last!" Appropriating his arm, she smiled brilliantly at him. He blanched visibly at the daggers shooting from her eyes. "Nothing will do but that I have a moment of conversation with my lord." She dug her nails into his coat sleeve and beamed at the round pink face of Miss Kitty Kirby at his side. "Do lend me his lordship for a few minutes, won't you, dearest creature? So kind!" And she swept away with him.

They proceeded up the stairs and stopped at the landing. Diana arranged herself prettily on a marble bench in full view of the bottom of the stairs, but effectively out of earshot of the rest of the assembly. She then glared up at Young George.

"Cad!" she spat. "Explain to me your crass and ungentlemanly conduct in divulging my secret! I had your solemn word, and you betrayed me utterly! How dare you! If I were a man I should call you out for this!"

Pomposity having deserted him in the face of her rage, Young George took refuge in the attitude he always adopted when being bullied by his father. "He got it out of me!"

"Cad!" she repeated scathingly. "First you browbeat the name out of me, then tattle to your father! And he of course can be relied upon to spread it to the four winds!"

"I could not help it," he pleaded. "You do not know my parent, Lady Diana. If he wishes to know something, he is as merciless as a hound after a fox!"

"Say rather a rabbit!" she retorted unkindly. "I hope you have had your little revenge by mortifying me so! To be the centre of every glance this evening! To be singled out by everyone in the room! To sit all evening next to that hen-witted countess, bored out of my mind, standing up not more than three times to dance, and with not even my betrothed here to sustain me!"

"Please believe me, I am most truly sorry . . ."

Diana was swept by a sudden wave of shame. She really had no right to use him this badly, since the initial deception had after all been hers. Still, she thought with a fresh access of fury, the whole world knew now, with heaven alone could predict what results. If only he had not blabbed the whole tale to his father! She opened her mouth to say as much when he stepped closer and leaned down, speaking in a pleading whisper.

"I beg you will not inform Lord Rushden of my error, Lady Diana. I should not like to have him angry with me for any reason, especially not for importuning his affianced lady."

Diana lost all sense of compassion for him and recoiled from him in disgust. "Oh, really, George!" she began, then sighed. What use? she asked herself morosely. The damage was done. She got to her feet. "Let us return now, if you please. I trust you will comprehend that I have absolutely no wish to address you in future if it can be at all helped. And I also trust that you will not offend me by speaking any more to me—or of me," she added pointedly.

"Your servant, my lady," he said, taking grateful refuge in the usages of civility.

"And how ill you have served me thus far!" she snapped, making it her parting shot as she swept down the staircase and back into the ballroom.

After receiving a dozen more congratulations from smiling faces with arching brows, her temples began to throb. As soon as it was decently possible, she begged her father to take her home. She had had enough of young men looking at her with betrayed eyes, young ladies who directed sly remarks at her from jealousy and from glee that she would no longer afford them any competition, and especially was she wearied of older ladies and gentlemen who insinuated that she would use her influence to curb Lord Rushden's deplorable habits and change his character.

Diana went directly to her rooms upon her return home, her head aching in earnest now. After Betsy had undressed her and brushed her hair, Diana dismissed her and collapsed across her bed to weep from sheer nervous exhaustion. A single, horrifying vision bedevilled her, and she sought respite from it in vain. But she could not stop conjuring the scene of Lord Rushden disgracing her in public.

Panic and despair were not, as a rule, Diana's way. She had been accustomed to directing her own life, and, through her regulation of his household, her father's, since the age of thirteen, when her mother had died. A succession of governesses had instilled in her the maidenly graces but not the sense of humility and subjugation to masculine rule deemed necessary to a young female's happiness. Indeed, every attempt to put her in awe of men only made Diana laugh, for she had successfully wound her father and all her male relations around her little finger since the cradle. Her father's friends found her delightful, and she learned from them how to modify the methods that had been so fruitful with her father into a charm that had placed so many of London's eligible young bachelors at her feet. Her experience of men, therefore, was primarily with those who scrambled to do her bidding, who considered her every word wonderful, and who gave her slightest wish the import of an imperial edict. Those who resisted her management—pleasant and subtle though it may have been—she simply ignored. And there had been few who had resisted.

Thus, as the sleepless night wore on, Diana began to reconsider her panic and to find it excessive. Surely she could bring this Lord Rushden around, as she had done so many young men. Positive of her attractions and certain of her ability to cozen his lordship into a solution palatable for both of them, she finally found slumber sometime before dawn and awoke five hours later with a zest for social battle she had not felt since an emigré French *duc* had paid her lavish court the previous season.

Her pleasure disappeared over the course of the next days. Each gathering at the homes of her friends became a trial by courtesy. Having been guilty of a medium-size deception, for so she had reduced it in her own mind, she now found herself enmeshed in a series of small untruths, each one carrying with it the threat of exposure.

She was asked innumerable questions about Lord Rushden and had good cause to bless horrid Lady Frewe for supplying her with his first name. When had they met? She did not recall, but she fancied it had been during her stay at Midfield. How had their acquaintance progressed? Slowly, she said with a smile. How had he proposed? Charmingly, . . . she simpered. When had he asked her to marry him? That was her secret, she replied archly. Where? Also her secret, with a more strained smile. How did she like his sisters (exceedingly), when was the wedding to be (whenever they could arrange it to the satisfaction of all concerned), how would she like being mistress of so fine a house as Midfield (prodigiously), did she not think him incredibly handsome (of course; although she still could not remember what he looked like, a fact she did not mention to her questioners). After three days Diana sat down and wrote out a list of the most frequently asked questions and her answers, and half-seriously considered having them printed up for general distribution.

She grew more adept at not quite answering, using the force of her smile and certain facial expressions to allow her interlocutors to assume what they wished. But the strain began to tell upon her nerves, for being fêted in all directions on the strength of a falsehood was not conducive to perfect mental harmony.

And she lived in constant fear that Lord Rushden would soon return to town and that someone else would see him before she had the chance to form his views on the subject of their engagement. Her only refuge and respite was in a long, despairing letter to Anne Rushden, her only hope in her friend's answer.

# 5

ATTENDANCE AT LORD Plowswyck's afternoon *pique-nique* on the lawns of his sprawling home was mandatory in the neighbourhood of Midfield, especially so that March, since joining the company would afford the local population a look at the two exiles. The scandal surrounding their removal from town having been duly reported by everyone's London connexions and fastened on with great relish, this local curiosity was held to be far more diverting than the more distant doings of persons but slightly known. Welcome, too, was the chance to be distinguished by either of the two dashing young officers, although this was purely an anticipation on the part of the young unmarried females of the area and scarcely approved by their mamas. Nonetheless, hairstyles were attempted and despaired of, dressmakers were driven to distraction, and maids succumbed to tears as they tried to make plain young ladies into London-style beauties.

The state of excitement was at its peak when the two young lords arrived fashionably equipaged, fashionably clad, and fashionably late. From the moment they escorted Lady Rushden and the four Misses Rushden from the east portico of Plowswyck House to the back lawns where the festivities were being held, the feminine flutter was all but audible. Certainly the two young men made a striking pair, each in elegant afternoon attire, Lord Hulme's dark good looks the perfect foil for the blondness of Lord Rushden. Their elaborately tied cravats were remarked upon, studied covertly, and would be copied the very next day by all young gentlemen with any pretense to fashion.

The *pique-nique* was a pretty sight, well organised by its host, eagerly attended by its guests, and congenial to all concerned. Long tables were set up near the house and groaned under the weight of cold chicken, ham, and beef. Small round tables were scattered about the lawns, which were in the first full flush of spring. Iced drinks were to be had at another table near the trees, and desserts were arranged at still another location. This separation of tables was a happy device for allowing the greatest possible interaction of the guests; on their trips for food or drink they could scarcely avoid each other, and many promising flirtations were begun or advanced at this annual event. That had been the pattern in the past. At this year's function no young men were to be watched or remarked upon but the two from Midfield Hall. And when into this colourful picture of country society came the Rushdens and their guest, all was complete and the day could truly begin.

Lady Rushden took her twin daughters over to several of their friends before settling herself beside Lady Plowswyck for a good long gossip. This left Roger, Anne, Michael, and Elizabeth, the last just returned from a visit to a cousin in Yorkshire, to stroll among the gathering, greeting friends and performing introductions for those who had not yet met Michael, and in general giving the assembly ample opportunity to observe and comment in their wake.

"For," as Anne murmured to Michael, "they will talk about you whatever we do, so we might as well do it right."

"Give them something to talk of, you mean?" he said and smiled. "Think of the risk to my reputation."

Roger snorted. "What reputation? I think we have given them quite enough time to look, Annie. And I did not think your vanity or Elizabeth's extended to such a display," he added with mock severity. "I am ready to call quits and fill a plate with some of the excellent food I see on those tables."

Elizabeth laughed softly, twirling her pale blue parasol to make the ribbons fly around her shoulders. "You always were a glutton," she chided. "Lord Hulme, you will not credit it, but I once saw him devour his own dinner, mine, Mary's and start in on Henrietta's—"

"A vile slander!" her brother cried. "You saw no such thing."

"I never doubt a beautiful lady's word—especially when I've

seen him go through half the Mess myself," Michael said, grinning. "And I pray you will call me Michael, Miss Elizabeth."

She turned to favour him with a smile, then swayed and went very pale. Michael grasped her arm to steady her.

"Oh," she said in a small voice, staring off at the company with large, glazed eyes. "He promised he would not come today!"

"Who?" Roger demanded.

Anne slipped an arm around her sister's waist. "Be easy, surely he will not speak to you."

"Will someone please tell me what mystery this is?" Roger asked.

"Oh, Roger, hush!" Anne hissed. "And smile, you know everyone is looking at us!" She turned to Michael. "Please take Roger to the refreshment table and bring back something cold for Lizzie."

"With all speed," he told her, obviously as bewildered as Roger but willing to do as she asked. He clapped his friend on the shoulder and they made their way to the table set up under the trees.

"What the devil—" Roger began, then nodded and smiled to the Misses Morris.

"Doubtless one of them will explain in time, but for now your sister needs a restorative."

When they returned, carrying not just glasses of cold lemonade but plates full of chicken and salad to the ladies, they found Elizabeth's colour much improved and her smile, though a trifle studied, firmly in place. Roger handed her a glass and, after she had sipped and thanked him, asked, "Now, Lizzie, what is all this about?"

Anne interrupted. "Michael, will you be so kind as to stay with Lizzie while I walk with Roger? Come along, darling brother," she concluded firmly, taking his arm and leading him away. "You idiot!" she exclaimed once they were safely out of earshot. "Has no one told you about Lizzie and Lord Gerald?"

"Gerald?" he repeated blankly. "I do recall Mama saying something to the purpose, but—"

"Lord preserve me from masculine blindness. The tale is this: Lizzie and Gerry are mad in love, and he is more or less promised to Lady Matilda—yes, your friend's half-sister. Now do you wonder why I wished to talk in private?"

"Matty? Good God, Annie, Lizzie's worth six of her! For all that Michael's my dearest friend, I don't have much opinion of his sister. Takes too strong after her mother, and the whole world knows what a snob the countess is."

"And what's that to the point when she and the earl have decided that Lord Gerald shall marry Matilda? Mama found out that Lizzie was meeting him this winter, and you never heard such a row."

"Has he been trifling with her?" Roger asked darkly. "For if he is cad enough to flirt with one girl while engaged to another—"

"Don't be such a prig!" She smiled, then trilled with laughter as a dowager hobbled past in the company of her two sons and four daughters, all of them unmarried and all of them admiring of the Rushdens. When they had passed, politely greeted and excused, Anne went on. "It would be just like you to fly into some brotherly rage over this. They met last summer before news of the engagement was noised about, and each was perfectly free. Of course, Gerry has very little money—"

"Why am I never consulted when my sisters contemplate matrimony?" Roger complained. "First Mary chooses someone I've never even met, and now Lizzie sets her fancy on this Lord Gerald person, whom I've never even heard of!"

"That's nothing to signify—I do wish you would listen, Roger! And pay attention. Mrs. Anning is waving to you from beside that tree."

He nodded, waved back, smiled, and looked at his sister again. "A plague on all these people. What about Lady Matilda?"

"She is here, of course, with her parents—sitting over there with Susan Routt. They arrived last night to stay—or weren't you listening to Lady Plowswyck when she welcomed Michael? Neither Lady Matilda nor Miss Routt condescend to address persons below their own station and dignity," she mimicked in an exact impersonation of Lady Matilda's high-pitched nasal whine.

Roger grinned. "She knows about Lizzie?"

"Certainly not, unless Gerry has been idiotish. Let us walk down to the river and I will tell you the whole."

"You mean there is more?"

"Hush!"

They took a path which led them away from most of the other guests, but of necessity met with persons engaged in similar promenades so that the conversation was interrupted at odd moments by the usages of civility.

"Though Gerry is one of the oldest names in the county, he hasn't all that much money, you see—oh yes, a lovely day, Mrs. Tottenhall!—and of course Lady Matilda has loads of it. He and Lizzie were afraid that Mama would consider him too poor—good afternoon, Miss Wilkerson, Mr. Durant, such a fine day, isn't it?—and that you'd think so, too. But they are most sincerely attached, Roger, and I do think that—Lady Harriet, do you know my brother? I shall surrender him to you directly, I promise, but he simply must see the new folly by the riverbank—and I do wish you'd settle a little something more on her. For them to be married is the only possible course, but only if she has a little more money and we can be rid of Lady—oh, Mr. Foley, you must come to tea soon at Midfield, Mama does so enjoy your poetry—well, Roger?"

He had listened to his sister's recital with astonishment, both at the tale she told and the manner of the telling. "This is all very interesting, Annie, but I don't really see the problem. It would seem to me that—how are you, Lord Chase? Yes, I shall certainly come by to look at your filly, very soon, I assure you—by which he means his daughter, of course," he added in an undertone to Anne. "What you are telling me is that Lord Gerald values the daughter of an earl for her money more than a Rushden for her love."

"Don't be so stuffy. Oh—there is Gerry, over by the willows. Do you not think him charming?"

He observed the gentleman in question, who was engaged in solitary and, by the droop of his shoulders, not very pleasant introspection. He was reasonably tall, with a broad though not stout figure and dark brown hair. "He looks well enough, and if Lizzie loves him—"

"She does!" Anne cried warmly.

"Oh, bother!" Roger exclaimed. "Here comes Lady Matilda, with Miss Routt in tow!" He put on his best smile as the two ladies approached. "Good day, my lady, Miss Routt. What a long drive you have had for one afternoon's entertainment!"

Lady Matilda allowed herself to smile. "We have been invited to spend the night at Plowswyck."

"Then we shall have the happiness of seeing more of you," Anne said sweetly. "And how is your dear father?"

"Not unwell, I trust?" Roger added.

"He is well, merely distressed at meeting my half-brother. As am I, truth to tell. Michael has upset my father the earl so completely that I scarcely know how to address him."

"Things will mend in time," Roger said blandly.

"I trust so, my lord. Good afternoon to you, Miss Rushden. Come along, Susan dear." They walked back up the path, muslins swaying.

Roger looked after them sourly. "How a man like Michael could have such a dowdy bore of a sister—"

"They are nothing alike, are they? She has none of his height, or his ease of manner—and his natural grace is missing in her as well," Anne observed as Lady Matilda stumbled while navigating a slight rise in the smooth pathway.

"Anne," Roger said thoughtfully, "I do believe you are in some danger."

"Of what?"

"Do you not listen to yourself, love?"

"May I not make comments about persons known to me without being thought in danger?"

"Not comments about Michael, you may not, without the danger of my thinking some very obvious things."

"Nonsense." Anne kept her colour but glanced away from him, which made him grin. "In any case, he and his sister are most unalike. That was the only point I was trying to make."

"Naturally," he agreed, and as she turned to regard him with a suspicious gaze, he wiped his face clean of all save a serious expression. "I am confirmed in every opinion I have had of her these ten years I have known her."

Anne was quiet for a moment, then said matter-of-factly, "You have mischief in mind, Roger. There is no mistaking that look. You might as well tell me, for I will find out anyway."

"Oh, I was merely wondering . . ." He pursed his lips thoughtfully, glanced at the morose figure of Lord Gerald, then went on. "What would happen, do you think, if Lady Matty were persuaded out of her match with Lord Gerald?"

Anne gave a little gasp. "Roger! You would not!"

He smiled slowly. "Would I not, now? With Michael's permission, of course. He doesn't like Matty above half, himself. But I was only speculating, my love." He grinned widely at her and took her hand. "Read me no lectures, Annie. I shall inform you of my scheme, if any. You are elected aide-de-camp in anything I undertake in the way of a campaign. Now, let us rejoin Lizzie and Michael. Surely she has recovered her spirits in his company. No one can remain unhappy around him for long, unless she is a young lady in love with him."

Anne began a heated retort, but Roger only laughed at her.

# =6=

ANY HOPES MICHAEL might have cherished about avoiding his father at Lord Plowswyck's were dashed the minute he saw his stepmother.

He usually had patience with her snobberies and pretensions, knowing full well that her main ambition in life was to see Matilda wedded to a peer. He did not discount the force of this ambition, or its probable success, for the countess's own mother had succeeded by marrying her to the Earl of Chetley.

The earl had married Michael's mother, the Lady Letitia, when she was only seventeen and he ten years older. Michael's birth a year later had cost her her health, and the confinement four years afterwards resulting in the birth of a daughter had cost her her life. The little girl had survived her by only a few weeks. Michael recalled his mother as only a delicious fragrance, silk dresses that rustled as she walked, and a velvet voice, although a full-length portrait painted the year of her marriage remained to show him that he had inherited her eyes. From the time he had been old enough to understand such things, he had known that his father had been passionately in love with his mother—but at about the same time as this realisation had come the earl's second marriage.

Michael had been quick to notice that his stepmother did not inspire similar devotion in the earl. It had been many years before he had comprehended that his father was one of those men who was meant to be married, and his second countess admirably suited his every requirement for a wife. She ran his castle elegantly, provided for his comforts, brought with her a substantial dowry, and gave him another child. That he did not love her was of no consequence to either of them, since she knew he had spent his heart on his first wife and did not much care. She had looks enough to entice his senses, although childbearing and overindulgence had spoiled much of the majesty of her figure, and the dizzying heights of nobility to which the former Miss Eleanor Baker had ascended had taken most of the easy charm of her manners and replaced them with hauteur. Still, Michael admitted in all fairness that she had made his father a good countess, and he suspected that the challenge of forcing the old line of nobility to accept a tradesman's daughter as his bride had greatly amused the earl.

Michael did not love and did not even much like his stepmother, but he quite understood her. In the interests of familial harmony he kept on good terms with her and with his half-sister, although his conduct towards the latter left much to be desired in her ladyship's eyes. She took no scruple in informing him of this now, after she had excused him from Elizabeth's company and directed him up to the house.

"The earl wishes to speak to you in private," Lady Chetley said. She never referred to her husband in any other manner than "the earl," just as her daughter rarely neglected to add the same reminder after every reference to her father. Long usage had accustomed Michael to this habit and most times he was able to ignore it, but just then it grated on his nerves. "He is very displeased with you, and Lord knows what effect this will all have on Matilda's chances in Society. I have written to everyone I could think of hoping to restore your credit, but the earl and I are both seriously distressed by your behaviour."

"I am indebted to you for your efforts on my behalf, but I am sure they will prove to be unnecessary," Michael said softly.

"Do not be absurd," her ladyship said, her dyed black ringlets bobbing as they ascended the steps and made for the drawing room where the earl waited for Michael. "What you do reflects upon us all, and I will not have you prejudicing Matilda's chances with your foolishness."

Ordinarily Michael would have shrugged off her words, but he was too nervous about meeting his father to speak cautiously. "If you think it my fault that Matty doesn't receive more invitations, my lady, you are mistaken,'' he snapped.

The ringlets bobbled in outrage. "She is but eighteen! Think upon the blight to her opportunities if you continue to behave in this fashion before Society!"

"I take leave to inform you, my lady, that while birth and fortune may recommend a woman, sweetness of character and largeness of mind will procure favour where other considerations fail. Think upon that, if you will be so kind. Now you must excuse me, for you cannot intend to keep my father waiting." He bowed, escaped into the coolness of the hallway, and took a moment to compose himself. Then, after securing from a footman directions to the drawing room where Lord Chetley was taking his ease, he went to the large oak doors and rapped lightly upon them.

"Enter!" the earl bellowed from within; his habitual volume was rarely short of a roar, but the force of that invitation made Michael wince. Closing the door carefully behind him, he approached the broad sopha where his father reclined with his foot up to nurse his gout.

The earl's attraction as a husband had not lain solely in his titles, wealth, and lands. Even at fifty-eight he was a magnificent figure of a man, although gout had crippled him and his hair had gone very grey. It was still a mane of curls very much like his son's, however, and the general physical resemblance was startling. Temperamentally, too, they were much alike, although Lady Letitia had imparted to her son much of her own sunny outlook on life and her grace of manner. The earl's usual expression was a frown.

He was not frowning as Michael advanced to the centre of the room and bowed. He instead regarded his son and heir with an amused, exasperated grimace.

"You wished to speak with me, my lord?" Michael asked respectfully.

"By God, boy, I did. What's all this about you and young Anne Rushden?"

Since his relationship with that lady was the last thing on his mind at present, Michael found himself blinking several times in astonishment, speechless for some minutes, and utterly bewildered. His father seemed oblivious to his difficulties and plunged ahead in a parade-ground shout. "Fine figure of a girl, Michael, but I can't help but wonder at your choice. Not much dowry, and too blasted many sisters! How far has it gone, eh? How did you propose? And she accepted, no doubt?"

Michael regained his powers of speech with an effort. "No—that is, I have not yet asked her—" He got thus far and no farther before his lordship rose painfully to his feet, limped over to him with the aid of a gold-topped cane, and dealt him a blow to the shoulder that would have felled a less muscular man.

"Don't like the idea of her being the next countess!" he cried. "I've heard tales of the goings-on at Midfield—mucking about in the gardens, so forth—and her behaviour at the last hunt was quite inappropriate. Did you hear about that, boy?"

"No, my lord."

"Hah!" The earl hobbled to a chair and sat down. "Riding like a man, first in on the kill. Matty was appalled. Mark my words, boy, that girl would make you the worst countess imaginable, bringing the family standards down beyond repair! She's a pretty thing, I'll grant you, but if you must have her, don't prattle of marriage. I'll increase your funds so you can make another arrangement—"

"That is enough!" Michael exploded. "I will not hear her spoken of in those terms, my lord! She will make the finest countess Chetley has ever seen, and I intend to make her so at the first opportunity! And I tell you to your head, your lordship, that it is not merely her beauty but her impeccable manners, her refined tastes, and her admirable character that make me love and esteem her! And if she is not bound by the conventions that make my sister so inestimably boring, so much the better! I shall marry Anne Rushden, my lord, will you nill you!"

The earl looked consideringly up at his son for a minute, then was taken with a fit of coughing. "Sit down, boy," he said in a much softer tone when he could speak again. "I always knew you'd marry the baggage. It's the only inclination of yours which I've ever entirely approved. Sit down, Michael!"

Michael gaped, but sat down.

"Now, about the dowry. God knows I've enough to set you up in whatever style you wish. You'll have Hulme House in London and

Boyden Lodge until I'm dead, of course, and then you'll live at Chetley—although you may have some shift getting Eleanor and Matty out. But I leave that to you. Has Rushden said what he'll give Anne?"

"You—you cannot mean you have no objection!"

"Don't be stupid, Michael!" the earl snapped. "She's the only girl I ever saw you with who's worthy of our name! I lived in horror for two years while you were sighing over that Lady Sylvie What's-her-name. My only fear now is that Anne will have the wit to refuse you."

"Alas, my lord, that is more than likely," Michael said glumly.

"What?" The dark blue eyes crackled with anger. "How have you offended her?"

"I have not—to my knowledge—that is—but she is so—" He stopped helplessly.

"Have you asked her?"

"Not yet."

"Then settle your mind. She won't refuse you if you do it right. You'd best wait until this latest business is over, though." The earl coughed again. "Get me a brandy, Michael."

He did so, worried by his father's grey pallour. "Are you quite well, my lord?" he asked anxiously as he extended a snifter of brandy.

"Never better." The earl took a healthy draught of liquor, his colour immediately improving. "Thought I wasn't going to mention this latest fiasco of yours, didn't you?"

"I apologise for any distress my actions may have caused your lordship," Michael said, his speech on this subject well rehearsed.

His father waved a fine hand. "Another of your ridiculous time-wasting escapades, but I think it will not signify once your regiment has need of you. Which won't be far in the future," he added grimly.

"You've had news?" Michael asked, leaning forward in his chair eagerly.

"Time in the country not to your liking, boy?" was the pointed observation. "Yes, I had it from a couple of old friends just yesterday morning. Boney's ripe for a fight in the Peninsula, and I expect Wellesley's making his plans this instant. So you can see where you and Roger won't be here much longer—and why I want to see you married to Anne before very long." The hard eyes softened. "I want a grandchild before I die, Michael. I want to see the eighth earl."

Michael replied gently, "The future seventh earl will be more than happy to provide, as soon as I can persuade Anne to marry me."

"Make it soon. Anything I can do to help?"

"Thank you, but no. Her feelings have altered in the past weeks, and I hope that soon we may reach an understanding."

"We'll hold the wedding in London," his lordship announced. "You'll be posted back there soon, I expect. What shall it be—St. Paul's?"

The future bride, all unaware of the plans being made in her honour, was at that moment seated in Lady Plowswyck's silver-and-orange boudoir. Anne rested comfortably from the heat while a maid stitched up a small tear in the hem of her dress. She was incredibly wearied of the ritual pleasantries attendant upon social affairs such as this one, and she had had more than enough of watching her sister Elizabeth's eyes avoid those of Lord Gerald. Idly she wondered if Roger could in truth manage to separate Lady Matilda from her notion of marrying Gerry; the thought was as amusing as it was scandalous.

"Did you not see, dearest Susan? Was it not precisely as I foretold?"

"Your brother is indeed thick as thieves with the whole family."

Anne, hearing this conversation emanate from the other side of the half-open hallway door, sat up straight with her eyes wide.

"And that insufferable sister positively doting on poor Michael, as if he had any opinion of her at all."

"One must suppose, Matilda, that he is kind to her for her brother's sake. He is so very good-hearted."

"But indiscriminate in his choice of friends. Will you attend to this curl, please, Susan? It should float—so. Yes. Such a shocking family altogether, wouldn't you say?"

"Indeed. Why, I even saw Miss Elizabeth Rushden half-swooning after your own Lord Gerald! But you will never guess what news I've had from my dear friend Lady Charlotte—you recall, my brother's wife's cousin, the daughter of the duke? Such a scandal about—"

"Scandal?"

At this critical juncture the two young ladies lowered their voices and moved off down the hall, their slippers making soft sounds on the parquet flooring. Anne swore under her breath. When the maid had finished, Anne got to her feet and went to the windows overlooking the lawns. She had no trouble picking out her brother's tall, fair-headed figure or, to her annoyance, Lord Hulme's dark curls. Heartily damning all men and especially those with odious sisters, she made a silent vow to remain a spinster and devote herself to good works and cats for the rest of her life.

But only after she had assisted Roger in captivating Lady Matilda, thereby freeing Lord Gerald to marry Lizzie—and only after she had shown the entire world a pleading Viscount Hulme on his knees before her.

Accordingly, after she had rejoined the company she sought out her brother and his friend, bestowed a dazzling smile on both, and earned a suspicious frown from Roger when she gathered all of them and invaded Lady Matilda's shady retreat under a chestnut tree. The battle was then joined in earnest.

# =7=

THE LADY MATILDA welcomed Roger's graceful advances—for he had read Anne aright and applauded her opening salvo—as if they were nothing less than her due. This irked him, for he was unaccustomed to a young lady being unaware of the distinction bestowed upon her by his fashionable notice. But he was not discouraged. For all her airs, she had not been much in Society, being barely eighteen years of age, and this worked to Roger's advantage. He spent the rest of that afternoon with her, letting it be known that he was wearied of the pace and pressure of life in town and longed for the quiet of the country—and the settled establishment to which any gentleman in his right mind aspired to most sincerely. Lady Matilda listened, commented, and received his attentions with the greatest presence of mind. He began to wonder by the day's end if she was taking his hints.

After consultation with Lady Rushden, an invitation was proffered and accepted, and all was arranged for Lady Chetley and her daughter to take luncheon at Midfield the next day. The excursion would add only a few miles to the return trip to Chetley Castle, although the meal was planned for an hour earlier than usual so that the guests would arrive back at their home before dark. The earl politely declined to attend, pleading estate business, but this did not overly trouble Roger, as Lady Matilda was his real aim.

Upon their return to Midfield, the ladies excused themselves from dinner and retired upstairs to their beds. Michael cornered Roger in the library and demanded an explanation of the marked favour shown to his half-sister. Roger only smiled.

"I find her most charming."

"Then it will be the first time you have done so these ten years," Michael said with a snort. "Are you feeling well, Roger?"

"Perfectly well, thank you," He selected a book from the shelves and stretched out on the sopha.

"You'll have the countess laying seige to Midfield," Michael warned.

"Perhaps we can arrange an exchange of prisoners in advance," Roger responded lazily.

Michael opened his mouth, closed it, and looked thoughtful. "You are the very devil," he finally said. "Anne told me about poor Elizabeth. Do you seriously propose to put yourself up as a candidate in place of Lord Gerald?"

"Your perspicacity amazes me." Roger yawned, and opened his book. "I am, after all, a somewhat better-feathered catch than Lord Gerald."

"Take care you are not plucked, roasted, and served with a sauce!"

"Michael!" Roger began to laugh. "You, who have observed me for years, have doubts now about my abilities?"

"I have seen you with ladies other than Matty. She'd throw over anyone less than a Royal Duke for the pleasure of hearing herself called Lady Rushden. I fear for your very life. How far has it gone?"

"I have tested her out, and I think it most promising, really. As you say, we have been acquainted with each other anytime these ten years, and it is most natural that I should suddenly notice she has grown to an interesting age." He smiled at his friend. "She is not attached to anything about Lord Gerald except his name and rank. If she had been, I would not embark on this campaign, I assure you. I am not so much of a blackguard as that."

"I never said you were," Michael replied irritably, pacing. "I only wonder how far you will take it."

"As far as needs must," he stated flatly. "Now go away, Michael, there's a good fellow. I am vastly involved with my book." And to prove it he settled it, opened, on his chest and closed his eyes to nap.

Michael fidgeted for some time, then walked outdoors. Their exile had passed pleasantly for the most part, with days spent riding about the vast estate, walking over well-loved paths, lazing in the sun, and retiring much earlier than was their usual wont. The calm and healthful country life had rapidly repaired damages that a constant round of late nights and excessive drinking inflicted on even the strongest young constitution, but placidity had begun to pall. Michael in particular felt the weight of his father's words about the situation in the Peninsula; he wanted to get back to town and prepare for the campaign that all knew was approaching. His trouble was that he also wanted very much to stay at Midfield and secure his position with Anne. So, torn between his need for action and the equally powerful need for an understanding with his chosen lady, his nerves were rapidly shredding.

He wandered out to the maze, not foolish enough to enter it despite years of familiarity with its tricks, and sat down on a small wooden bench. Twilight had settled its gentle folds over the hills, softening all sounds so that the river, a quarter of a mile down the grassy slopes, spoke more distinctly than at any other time of day. Michael lingered, half-dreaming, and lost track of time.

Anne wandered, too, though on the other side of the house and with even more troubled thoughts. She had retired to her room with every intention of changing into her nightdress, having a bowl of soup, and going to bed. But on her dressing table she found a letter from Diana, which had been misdirected and had taken close to a fortnight to reach her. Anne eagerly ripped open the seal and read hurriedly, but the contents of the letter so agitated her feelings that she abandoned her original plan and slipped outside into the sweet evening air to think. She pulled the pages from her pocket and, choosing her favourite spot in the herb gardens, composed herself to read again.

> *Dearest Anne,*
> *I scarcely know where to start. I am disgraced, ruined, humiliated—in short, I am found out! If you are still my Friend after you have read this, you are truly the Sweetest and most forgiving creature alive. For I deserve every calamity of loss of regard and respect which*

*can befall me.*

Anne paused in her reading to shake her head. This was Diana at her most dramatic, and Anne had learned to halve most of her friend's reports in order to discover the truth of them. In humorous prose, this facility of Diana's was a happy one, designed to entertain and delight, but in graver concerns it was inappropriate. Yet as Anne read on, she could not help but fret anew at the seriousness of the situation described.

> *You will recall my last letter telling you with all good humour of my borrowing your Brother for a night's fictitious engagement? Well, to be brief, Young George tattled the whole to his father, who of course could not be relied upon to keep secret an impending Invasion of France, let alone so trivial a thing as an Engagement. The results you can imagine. I am congratulated from every corner, toasted without end, and constantly asked when Lord Rushden will be returned to Celebrate officially with me. My Father is tireless on the subject. My modiste is planning my wedding dress and trousseau! But all this will be Nothing to what will occur when your Brother comes to London, which he must shortly do, as I have heard that Wellesley is planning the Campaign.*

Anne winced. Roger would be livid. Public humiliation would be the least of Diana's punishments for using Roger so. Anne set one part of her mind to disentangling them with as little damage as possible to each while she reread the rest of the letter.

> *I am distrait, Anne, I cannot sleep and I am loath to show my face, and this when I am supposed to be the Happiest of females. I must go to parties and balls, smile, laugh, and play the happy Bride, when I desire nothing more than to hide in my rooms and never show my face again.*

This was discounted as an excess of dramatics, although it showed Anne the extremes of Diana's desperation. She sighed.

> *My dearest Anne, if you can begin to forgive my stupidity, then please find some way of coming to me At Once. I need your support and your good Sense in these horrid days. I am selfish to beg this of you, since I know how much you love Midfield and how its attractions have increased since the arrival of Lord Hulme, who is a most Charming gentleman (I have met him once or twice at Almacks). Yet in the name of our Friendship I beg you to come to me as soon as may be.*
>
> *My fondest love to you and your family as always, and I plead with you to have pity on your affct.*
>
> *Diana*

Anne folded the pages and put them in her pocket once more. The plea of her presence could not but touch her deeply; a letter to a trusted friend is a poor substitute for that friend's bracing presence, and Anne felt keenly that she should start for town at once. Considering the date of the letter and its receipt by her only today, heaven alone knew what agonies Diana had endured in the time between.

She sat for a long while gazing at the magnificence offered by Midfield at twilight. But not even the velvet spread of lawns to the trees or the scents borne on the spring air could distract her from her thoughts. Too many insoluble puzzles crowded her mind—Lizzie and Lord Gerald, Diana and Roger, Roger's schemes about Lady Matilda, and—Michael.

"Anne! I thought you too fatigued to leave your room."

She started and blushed as the object of her most disturbing thoughts appeared before her. "I am not so tired as Mama and Lizzie and the twins," she managed, then recovered her self-possession and went on. "What do you here, my lord?"

"'My lord'?" Michael smiled in the gathering gloom, walking closer to her. "How formal! I am but admiring the view."

"It is lovely, is it not?" she replied automatically.

"Yes," he said softly, looking directly at her and paying no attention whatever to the other charms of the evening. "May I—?"

She made room for him on the bench, and he sat down. "Did you enjoy our country society today, Michael?"

"More than I thought I would," he admitted. "And I learned some tales of Roger from Elizabeth that should keep him squirming for weeks."

She laughed, but as the dusky light grew dimmer around them she grew unsettled. She had sat thus with other young men and not felt this way at their proximity. She suddenly recalled their first meeting, when she had been barely fifteen and dazzled by the handsome young officer her brother had introduced as his dearest friend. Swiftly she refused the memory. Yet the feeling persisted, and she realised that of all the young men she had ever known, Michael was the only one who had never bored her. Even when she was furious with him, even during those years when she had avoided his company, she had always found the mere mention of him stimulating.

Yet she could not help wishing that he would not look at her in that earnest way, his dark blue eyes exactly the colour of the evening sky over the western hills. To talk with him, even to argue with him, was the only reason she liked having him near her, she told herself sternly. She had no desire to see his face look thus.

"Anne," he murmured.

"Oh!" The exclamation escaped from her involuntarily as he made the single syllable of her name into something closely resembling an endearment. She looked wildly around her, control nearly lost, and saw a familiar figure steal from the house and walk swiftly round to the riverside. "Oh!" she said again, more composedly this time, "there is poor Lizzie, walking all alone. I cannot thank you enough for keeping her company and distracting her mind from Lord Gerald today, although take care you do not fall in love with her, for she is a darling and the best sister I could ever hope for."

"Anne," Michael said severely, "you are exactly like Roger. He babbles like a brook when he's nervous. What is the trouble?"

"Nervous?" she echoed. Then she rose to her feet, cursing the part of her that wished to stay near his warmth, and smiled down at him. "I am chattering to keep my teeth from clacking together with the cold. Lizzie was sensible enough to get a shawl to wrap herself with, but I was not so wise. I must go in before I catch a chill."

Thus she escaped, but with the uneasy feeling that Michael had seen right through her. Yet that emotion was superceded by the sudden thought that Roger had said Michael was in love with her. She tried to laugh as she brushed out her hair for the night, but her fingers trembled so that she had to throw the heavy silver brush down. She glared at her reflexion in the long glass, daring herself to believe Roger's words. Michael was no more in love with her than—than Roger was with Diana.

Anne was still rational enough to know that sleep that night was an impossibility. She dressed in a plain gown and made her way downstairs to the kitchens, where she lit enough candles to make the warm room blaze like daylight. Her excess of energy she used in the baking of a dozen pies. Halfway through the making of the crusts her sister Elizabeth joined her and together they worked through half the night. When they had tested the heat of the oven and found it satisfactory, they sat over a pot of strong sweet tea while the pies baked. Elizabeth was not inclined to conversation, which suited Anne; she could not have offered her sister any hope regarding Lord Gerald and was too confused in her own mind about Michael to have much to say.

The scent of baking apples and raisins brought the twins down to enquire sleepily what was going on at this hour of the night. Catherine and Caroline were enlisted to help tidy the kitchen, but soon all four lost any pretensions to being termed fashionable young ladies when Elizabeth suddenly decided to lead them in a flour fight. This noisy activity brought their brother, handsomely disheveled in his dark green dressing gown, to the kitchen door to demand the meaning of the uproar. He was immediately pelted with fistfuls of flour from four directions at once.

Bellowing, he scooped Catherine up in one arm and Elizabeth in the other, threatening to roast them along with the pies if they did not recall their age and station at once. Caroline and Anne, still free, dumped an entire bowl of flour on his head and he collapsed, sputtering and white from hair to shoulders. He was about to retaliate when Elizabeth gave a little cry and rushed to remove the pies from the oven, and within a few minutes they were all seated around the long table, drinking tea and happily devouring the new-baked treat.

Anne watched Roger with a smile, finding little trace of her elegant brother in the man who stuffed apple pie into his mouth and seemed perfectly unaware of the white-dusted ruin of his dressing gown. She recalled suddenly the fifteen-year-old baron who, flushed with his own importance, had attempted to lecture his six sisters on propriety; their response had been to pelt him with pillows until the drawing room was awash in feathers. She wished suddenly that those happy, uncomplicated times could return, when they had teased and plagued and adored their only brother. But as the kitchen was at last set to rights and they had kissed each other good night and sought their beds, Anne realised it was not the past she wished for, but a future in which her own children would play equally silly games with each other. She wanted her own home and family, her own small happy world of cats and gardens and pies, of laughing little girls and grinning little boys.

It was a sweet, disturbing longing, and she could not rid herself of it even in sleep, where all the children she knew to be hers had Michael's black curls and blue eyes.

# 8

IT PROVED SINGULARLY difficult for Roger to detach Lady
Matilda from the rest of the party the next day at luncheon. Lady
Chetley, who fancied herself a woman of the world and who chose
to ignore the two stone she had added to her figure since her
marriage, monopolised Roger for her own satisfaction for the
whole of the time before the meal. At table he was seated next to
her, with the object of his campaign well down the expanse of
linen-covered mahogany, barely visible between vases filled with
spring roses. But Roger bided his time and was rewarded when they
all adjourned to the back lawn for cool drinks and conversation.

The talk was charming and pointless, but Roger attached himself
to Lady Matilda's side and began to advance his cause. No young
lady vastly in love with another man—or even with that man's
great name—could look as Matilda did when Roger complimented
her on the cunning way her bonnet ribbons were tied. Likewise, no
young lady committed to one gentleman could take so much
enjoyment in the company of another or react with such obvious
pleasure to a turn about the gardens. Roger selected a pink rose and
presented it to her, saying it was a close approximation to the
colour of her cheeks.

In short, the Rushden charm worked its way toward Lady
Matilda's downfall, and only two people besides Roger himself
knew what he was doing and why. While Anne was half-amused,
half-appalled at this new side of Roger, which she was seeing for
the first time, Michael's amusement was tempered with irritation,
for he had very little desire to listen to his stepmother's furies when
Roger proved to be unavailable. Lady Rushden watched in be-

wilderment; the twins, in awe, all the while telling each other that any young man wishing to attach either of them had better have speeches just as pretty as their brother's; and Elizabeth seemed oblivious to the whole farce.

It grew time for the Chetley visitors to leave, but no one made mention of the lateness of the hour until it became inpossible to think of starting out. Thus the dearest wish of Lady Chetley was fulfilled: an invitation to stay the night at Midfield was extended and eagerly accepted. A note was dispatched to the earl advising him of the plan; trunks were taken down from the carriage; rooms were assigned. Michael escaped as soon as he could decently do so and went down to the riverbank to breathe air not tainted by his sister's simpers and his stepmother's snobberies.

Some years earlier, on a long summer visit to Midfield, he and Roger had spent a great deal of time and effort creating a fishing and swimming pond in a bend of the river, just out of sight of the house. Michael went there now, seeking the quiet in which to brood further about Anne. But he was not the first visitor, and when he saw a golden head above a green-striped dress his heart gave a most distressing leap in his chest. Then the lady turned slightly and he saw that it was not Anne, but Elizabeth. She stood quite still for some time on the bank. He hesitated, then was about to call out to her, hoping he could once again distract her from her melancholy, but just then she gave a little cry and began to run lightly across the grassy slope.

Hulme gasped as he recognised the man toward whom Elizabeth ran: Lord Gerald. Michael averted his eyes from their rendezvous, as any gentleman should, and hunkered down on his heels while he pondered what to do. On the one hand, it would be most unkind in him to interrupt their meeting; on the other, he had Elizabeth's honour to think of. And, additionally, the man was more or less betrothed to his own sister. Honour battled with feeling for a few minutes, and then he got to his feet. Making a ridiculous amount of noise, he made his way through the undergrowth to the riverbank where Elizabeth had originally stood. As he had ardently hoped, Lord Gerald had disappeared and the only person he met was Elizabeth, who, though flushed and bright-eyed, greeted him without a single tremor in her voice or face.

"Good afternoon, Michael," she said, smiling at him.

"I find more and more attractions in the solitary places of Midfield," he commented, taking her arm. "One is likely to find a charming young lady in each." They strolled for a time, chatting idly. Yet Michael knew she wished another at her side, and, being in roughly the same position himself, his heart was in perfect charity with hers.

When they returned to the house, Roger and Anne were waiting for them, the former to ask a few moments of his friend's time, the latter to take her sister off for yet another of their mother's planning sessions for Henrietta's and Mary's weddings. They separated in the hall, but Roger had advanced no farther than a few steps to the library before he said, "Michael, old man, would you have any objections to my suing formally for your sister's hand?"

"What?" Michael roared, his volume adequately covering the gasps that issued from the two young ladies at the foot of the stairs.

"In all good faith, I assure you," Roger went on.

The sisters' differing reactions may be imagined: Elizabeth's eyes lit with hope, Anne's with alarm. Each stopped in her tracks to listen further, but the library door had closed and they were left to stare at each other in silence. Finally Elizabeth came out of her trance and ran upstairs.

Anne was slower to recover. The choice between her sister's happiness and her brother's was a cruel one, for she loved both deeply. Lady Matilda would never make Roger happy, but Lizzie and Lord Gerald had already found their happiness in each other. Should she allow this mad plan of Roger's to go forward, thus securing her sister's marriage, or should she foil the scheme and trust to Lord Gerald's feelings to give him the courage to break off with Lady Matilda? Anne deliberated for long, agonised minutes, and then turned and hurried up the stairs.

After a dinner during which Anne, Michael, and Elizabeth stayed silent and Roger, Matilda, and the countess talked incessantly, Anne was grateful for the time spent alone by the ladies in the drawing room. She needed the moments away from her brother in order to compose her thoughts. She could not watch Lady Matilda's blooming spirits or listen to her high-pitched laughter, for her own agitation made that lady's looks and voice unbearable, but at least they were better than Roger's insufferable charm. Anne longed to consult with Michael but did not dare; she had no way of knowing whether he would prove an ally to her or stay loyal to Roger. And as she glanced again and again at Lady Matilda, she marvelled that the same father could have produced two such different offspring. Where Michael's eyes were wide and fine, with long lashes and a disarming twinkle in their depths, Matilda's were paler, narrower, sharp-gazed and scantily lashed. Michael's riotous black curls were, on Matilda, lank and frizzed around her face, and bones that in his countenance were proud were in hers haughty. And as for their characters—nothing could be more wholly opposed than Matilda's superciliousness and Michael's sunny good humour. Anne shuddered inwardly at the thought of her brother being married to someone like Matilda, and her disquiet of spirit grew almost unbearable.

And yet—there was Lizzie to think of, Lizzie who had sat silently through the meal and who tucked herself away in a corner now, her eyes misted with dreams. Anne could not choose which to make unhappy, and she knew that the outcome depended solely upon her.

When Michael and Roger joined them, she cursed her brother roundly for choosing a seat next to Lady Matilda, an album in his lap, for an intimate *tête-à-tête*. Anne picked up her embroidery and sat nearby, listening without shame to the conversation. Every so often she would catch Michael's gaze from across the room where he wrote to his father; his eyes were worried and puzzled.

"My sisters have been plaguing me this age to look at their handiwork," Roger was saying to Matilda. "But I have never found the time or the right company in which to appreciate it."

"Your sisters are all very talented, my lord."

"I do wish you would call me Roger," he invited, making Anne wish that it were possible to strangle one's brother with impunity.

"Then you must also use my name," Lady Matilda replied, a concession that almost made Anne's eyes pop. She looked steadily down at her needlework, biting her lips.

"Ah, but would Lord Gerald like that?" Roger asked, concern in his voice.

"Lord Gerald?"

"I have heard nothing definite, but I understand that congratulations are shortly to be offered to that fortunate gentleman."

"You have heard prematurely, Roger," Matilda said primly, and the album snapped shut. "While it is true that a match has been talked of, and my father the earl and my mother have no objections, I myself am far from decided on the subject. I beg you will tell me who is spreading rumours about me."

"But I hear it from all quarters!" Roger exclaimed. "Still, I am very glad to know—that is to say, I think it most—what I mean is . . ."

Anne was ready to stuff her embroidery, frame and all, down her brother's throat. Lady Matilda, however, seemed vastly taken with the conversation. Any well-bred young lady would have turned the talk at this point, the salient facts having been given and understood on both sides. Anne listened sourly to the ensuing speeches, grudgingly admitting to herself that she could hardly fault the girl for wishing to continue this interesting line of talk with a handsome, unmarried peer.

"One is spoken of whether one wishes it or no," Lady Matilda observed disapprovingly. "I myself place very little credence in gossip, but I must admit that it is shocking to hear one's supposed engagement talked of when one had not decided upon the thing."

This last made Anne smile, just a little, as her brother agreed heartily with Lady Matilda's view. Having heard quite enough, Anne set her needlework aside and, approaching the pair, smiled charmingly. "I am in the mood for some music, and I have heard it said that you play most delightfully, Lady Matilda. You will favour us, will you not? We have a fine instrument, but alas, none of us is capable of rendering so much as a scale correctly in tune."

Roger shot her an annoyed look and she ignored it. Eager to show off her talent, Matilda readily acquiesced, and thus Anne had the satisfaction of removing her from Roger's company for the rest of the evening. She stood beside her, turning the pages, glad for her own sake that Lady Matilda did indeed play very well, for there was nothing worse than a badly played pianoforte, in Anne's mind. It was the simplest thing in the world to stay at Lady Matilda's side when the party broke up, and simpler even than that to join her on their walk up the stairs.

Roger observed all this with no small amount of suspicion. It was not like Anne to dissemble so. It occurred to him that she might be helping to further his cause, but if that were so, why had she curtailed so promising a conversation? For he had no doubts that she had listened to every word.

Puzzled, he sought refuge in the library for a solitary brandy and thought. And his thoughts were pleasant. His vanity had been soothed by Lady Matilda's behaviour at Midfield, and he had convinced himself that her attitude at Plowswyck was simply coyness coupled with a consciousness of the eyes of the neighbourhood on them. Certainly the acquaintance had progressed with startling rapidity in the last two days. He smiled. Proposing to her would neatly solve a number of problems. Elizabeth and Lord Gerald could be formally betrothed, for one thing. Lady Matilda would have a spectacular catch to display in London, and would certainly not be heartbroken at his demise—for he had ascertained many years ago that she had very little heart to break. His own mother would be pacified. Her mother would be ecstatic. And one of his sisters could provide the next Lord Rushden from among their progeny—perhaps even a son of Anne and Michael's. It entirely suited him that a son of his favourite sister and his dearest friend should inherit. And since the direct male line would be broken, perhaps the curse would not be visited upon the twenty-ninth baron as it had been on the previous twenty-eight.

He heard all at once the echo of Anne's cry from the heart that he should not marry without love. Well, he would not, he reasoned; he simply would not marry at all. Lady Matilda would do him very nicely as a fiancée. He had explained as much to Michael that afternoon, though not all his motives had entered the conversation. He smiled again at recalling Michael's horrified expression; it had not been easy, but he had at last resigned his friend to the scheme, and whereas Michael did not approve in the slightest, he would make no objection. Roger reviewed his plans, finished his brandy, and went to his bed with a smile on his lips.

Experience of women had not altered the conceit fostered in Roger from childhood by six fond sisters and an adoring, if stern, mother. Each of the ladies most intimately connected with him, moreover, had sufficient differences of character and taste to have given him a fair understanding of the working of the female mind before he was even out of short coats. Henrietta, nearest to him in age, was wholly content to spend her entire life in the country with her horses, her dogs, her hunting, and a husband of exactly the same inclinations. Mary, next eldest, had a zest for cataloguing which during girlhood had found employment in listing every stick of furniture, chip of porcelain, and brushstroke of oil paints to be found in Midfield; this had translated into a passion for genealogy that would find ample satisfaction in the stable of racehorses bred by her future spouse. These two pretty, uncomplicated ladies had taught Roger the direct paths to dealing with women.

Anne, socially accomplished and yet with her heart truly in the country life, could preside over a midnight baking spree, a dinner for ninety, or a fox hunt with equal good humour and taste. She was the most complex of his sisters, but he understood her very well; for all her variety of activities, she was as singlehearted as the elder two, and he had known for years she was eventually going to marry Michael. Still, she had to be handled with much more care than Hetty or Mary, and frequent conflicts had taught him how to tread gently.

Elizabeth was the quietest of the girls, the most studious, and the one Roger understood only sketchily. Her mysteries intrigued him, and from her he had learned to listen to what a woman had to say in order to discover her true character, which might be hidden beneath layers of deceptively calm manners. He had made the mistake only once of assuming Elizabeth's feelings to be less strong than those of the rest of their outspoken family, and the hurt he had caused her then was something he never wished to repeat with any woman.

The twins were total opposites to each other. Catherine's shyness in company was countered by a tendency to chatter in private, but she was always eclipsed by the vivacious, flirtatious Caroline. From this pair he had learned much about the delights of the young and unformed female mind, how to please them best, how to amuse them and keep them in awe while retaining their affection.

And then there was his mother. Widowed at the absurdly young age of seven-and-twenty, she had been the benevolent autocrat of his childhood and was the often-ignored conscience of his manhood. She was proud, still beautiful, and devoted to the family her lord had given her. Roger found in his mother the model for feminine constancy, however little he relished her strictures on his behaviour.

Among the seven of them, then, Roger had known every type of teasing, indulgence, scolding, severity, tenderness, and support available to a man—except for that combination of passion and sweetness that is usually termed love. His knowledge of women, therefore, despite his wide experience of mother, sisters, aunts, cousins, decorous flirtations, and mistresses, remained incomplete.

He did not know this, of course. He trusted to his instincts, honed by years of accomplishment and confirmed with his every success, to serve him well in his coming encounter with Lady Matilda. He had every expectation of emerging victorious from a battle in which she had not a chance.

His opportunity arose the next morning as the house prepared for the departure of the guests. Roger met Lady Matilda quite by accident in the upper hallway and, blessing his luck, drew her into a small alcove made appropriately romantic by the sunlight streaming through a stained glass window depicting St. George on horseback.

"My lord!" she exclaimed as he took her hand and placed a finger gently to her lips to enjoin her to silence. Her expression grew even more astonished as he took both her hands, seated her on a gilt chair beneath the window, and went down on one knee.

"It cannot have escaped you that in the past days I have become more and more captivated by your conversation, your character, and your person," he said rapidly, as if fearing to be interrupted. "I cannot tell you how glad I was to hear that your rumoured engagement to Lord Gerald was nothing more than a rumour indeed.

Because, my dearest Matilda, only you can make me the happiest of men.''

She gaped at him, her pale blue eyes agog. Encouraged, Roger kissed her fingertips.

"Matilda,'' he began, but in the instant she freed her hands and dealt him a slap across the cheek with a force that would have done credit to a horse.

"Cad!'' she cried, leaping to her feet. "Scoundrel! I shall never speak to you again—no, not even if my father the earl commands me to it! How dare you!''

"Matilda!'' He reached out to catch her as she tripped over the leg of the chair, but she righted herself without assistance and glared down at him.

"To trifle with the affections of one lady while secretly engaged to another! You are reprehensible, my lord, and I will have no more to do with you!'' She squeezed past him in the narrow confines of the alcove. "Your poor sister, white with shame as she was, told me the whole of it last night! Be assured, my lord, I would not marry you if you were the last man on earth!''

She was gone down the stairs in a flurry of muslin. Roger got slowly to his feet, one hand to his stinging cheek. Profoundly bewildered, he shook his head to clear it. "What have I done amiss?'' he wondered aloud. And then, recalling her ladyship's last comments, threw his head back and roared out, *"Anne!"*

# === 9 ===

THE DOWAGER DUCHESS of Sturbrough's monthly dinner for her family—an intimate gathering of not less than sixty on any given occasion—was strictly for blood relatives, their husbands and wives, and those offspring capable of keeping their mouths shut so as not to irritate Her Grace's nerves. Any of her several score relations who, being in London on the fifth of each month, did not attend was visited on the morning of the sixth by Her Grace's personal physician, since it was to be assumed that that relation was on his or her deathbed.

A handwritten invitation arrived on the first day of April requesting the presence of Lord Bellrose and his daughter at Blackhearst House for the duchess's monthly entertainment. It took Lord Bellrose some minutes to recall that the duchess was Lady Rushden's elder sister, and his confusion on receipt of the invitation turned to pleasure. Diana took a little less time to recall that Anne had mentioned Her Grace as an aunt, and her confusion gave way to panic.

On the evening of the fifth she changed her ensemble five times, dreading the parade for formal approval of Lord Rushden's relations. Finally, half an hour late and with her father bellowing from the foot of the staircase for her to present herself to him upon the instant, she emerged from her room in the formidable armour of leaf-green silk and her mother's diamonds. A last quick glance in the hallway mirrors confirmed her confidence; let the old cats howl, she thought defiantly. She was ready for them, although her colour left a little to be desired.

It was a warm, moonlit evening, deliciously clement for April, filled with stars and accented by the sweet music of the household orchestra. Diana advanced in the receiving line to do battle, but found to her surprise that the various Sturbroughs, Rowes, Cresseys, Farnsworths, and assorted other names and titles were uniformly charming people who commented not at all on her engagement to their dashing bachelor scion. She guessed correctly that since the formal announcement had not as yet been made, they were taking no official notice of the situation, although that did not preclude treating her as one of the family. Since neither her father nor her mother had any living relatives, and she herself was an only child, she found the profusion of aunts, uncles, cousins, nieces, nephews, and more complicated connexions to be interesting, if confusing. And as dinner progressed she found that she enjoyed their company—or at least she enjoyed the thirty or so she had met out of the ninety-two in attendance.

The evening passed with remarkable charm. After the gentlemen rejoined the ladies in the three vast drawing rooms, which had been opened to connect with each other, it was suggested that so fine a night ought not go to waste. So the outer doors were opened in order that dancing might commence on the terrace. Diana saw her father pleasantly occupied in a card game, accepted the hand of some Rushden cousin or other, and joined one of the sets. She swayed gracefully in time to the music, conversing now and again with her partner, half-dreaming in the romantic atmosphere scented with lime and orange, roses, thyme, and a hint of lavender.

When the dance ended she smiled at the young Cressey who had partnered her and went back into the drawing room to seek a refreshing glass of champagne. As she entered there was a stir in the room, and Diana had that moment of embarrassment one feels when suspecting that conversations have been interrupted by the entrance of their subject. But no one was looking at her; all eyes were turned to the doorway, and after a moment a pathway opened from it to where Diana stood transfixed. A tall, lean young man of about thirty, broad-shouldered in his uniform coat, which was crossed by the Order of the Bath, his golden hair smoothly in place, advanced towards her. He wore a pleasant smile, but his eyes snapped with sardonic amusement. Diana went crimson to the low décolletage of her gown, and his eyes followed the progress of her blush with insolent interest. In her first rage of panic, all Diana could think was that he was impossibly handsome and no one should have eyes that blue.

"Good evening, my dear." Lord Rushden bowed elegantly over her hand. "I had so hoped to give you the meeting tonight, and it seems Providence has blessed me." He straightened and looked down at her with a devilish glint in his eyes.

"Good evening, my lord," she managed, her throat so tight with terror that the words very nearly strangled her.

"I must introduce you formally to my Aunt Sturbrough," he went on, taking her arm firmly and leading her to the gilt chair in the corner where the duchess held court.

Diana was borne along on legs that at first would barely hold her, and she was more than grateful for the strong arm that supported her. But as they passed among the groups of silent, staring relations, her spine stiffened. She smiled brilliantly as Lord Rushden bent to kiss his aunt's cheek.

"Here you are at last, loathsome boy," Her Grace grumbled. "Where have you been? I have been waiting for you this age."

"My horse cast a shoe on the way from Midfield, Aunt. I am most grievously sorry to have kept you waiting."

"High time you put in an appearance. This poor child has been running the gauntlet all alone." A wrinkled hand, loaded down with rubies, patted Diana's arm. "You may kiss me, child."

She bent to do so, her heart pounding wildly, her cheeks burning. "Everyone has been most kind, Your Grace," she murmured.

"And what do you think of my fiancée, Aunt?" Lord Rushden asked conversationally.

Diana almost staggered but with a supreme effort kept herself steady and smiling.

"Exactly what you want in a wife," the duchess pronounced. "Now, leave me and go talk by yourselves. I've had the library reserved for your private greetings."

"Excellent idea, Aunt—and thoughtful as always. Come along, my dear Diana."

They walked the length of the three huge rooms, Diana with her hand resting lightly on Lord Rushden's arm, gathering smiles and nods as they went. Down the hallway and into a book-lined room they walked in absolute silence, and at last Diana was seated on the edge of an armchair, her skirts flowing delicately around her, her spine straight as a plumb line. Lord Rushden left the door open a few inches, crossed to the fireplace, and leaned against the mantel with his arms folded. As she looked up at him she saw to her dismay that not only was he much handsomer than she had originally thought, but he was also much angrier than his eyes had originally betrayed. They smouldered now, his lips drawing into a thin, grim line as she stayed silent. Diana squared her shoulders and opened her mouth to speak.

"Pray don't bother with an apology," he said rudely. "I'm quite sure you're not sorry. How diverting it must be for you to play out this farce of an engagement with me!" He laughed sharply. "Why was I so honoured, incidentally?"

"Yours was the first name I could think of," she replied irritably. "My father wanted to marry me to that fool of a Young George—"

"Young George?" he interrupted.

"Lord Fonteville's son. I refused to marry him."

"Fortunate man!"

"You are insulting, my lord!"

He inclined his head in a mocking little bow. "I cry your pardon, my dear—especially after you have so complimented me by making me the object of your favours. Do go on with your story. I so enjoy fairy tales."

"Try to see it as I did!" she exclaimed angrily. "Commanded by my father to marry that—that—"

"Words fail you," he supplied helpfully.

"I could not persuade that imbecile that we were utterly unsuited for each other, and I had to think of something! Heaven alone knows why I struck upon your name—no doubt you will ruin me and take the greatest delight in your revenge."

He regarded her with raised brows for a moment, then casually flicked a nonexistent piece of lint from his sleeve. "I have not the slightest intention of denying our engagement, Lady Diana."

The fan she carried snapped in two.

"As it happens, it suits me very well to be engaged at present," he continued easily. "The reasons need not concern you, I think. Any young lady of quality would have done—you as well as any." He grinned at her. "Since you have so happily anticipated my need, I can only thank you for your timely masquerade—I think I need not say your timely lie." After a brief laugh he went on. "I think a few months of association will suffice, and after that we can invent a quarrel and go our separate ways. I am really most grateful to you, Lady Diana."

She merely gaped at him.

"It is a most equable match," he went on with a calm that maddened her. "Our stations are equal, we both possess land, money, and a good name, and it cannot but help that you are reasonably attractive. A man like me cannot be expected to affiance himself to an antidote, after all." He grinned as she gave an outraged splutter. "And doubtless your charms are more than physical. It requires a highly original mind to hit upon so novel a scheme for ridding oneself of an unwanted suitor. I think you and I shall deal famously together."

With great difficulty she bit back a shriek of fury. Taking two very long breaths, she rose to her feet and swept him a deep curtsey. "I am so pleased," she purred with deadly sweetness, "that your plans fall in so well with my own. Thank you for being so convenient, my lord." She turned and would have left the room, but he was beside her in an instant and caught at her arm.

"You little fool! If you storm out of this room looking like that, it will be all over town by noon tomorrow that we have quarrelled! Have a little more sense! If we are to carry this off, you will have to learn to control your temper and your tongue!"

"Let me go!" She struggled in vain against his iron grip.

"Not until you are willing to act the part of my loving bride!"

They glared at each other for some seconds. Finally she wrested her arm from his grasp. "Gladly, my lord," she jeered. "Only pray you instruct me on your notions of decorum! Shall you take me for daily airings in the park? Attend on my every movement? Pick up my fan, call at teatime to discuss our wedding? And I—shall I embroider your initials on handkerchiefs, send you *billet-doux*? Do you wish me to blush when you enter a room and repine when you are absent?'' She snorted. ''God! How consumingly boring!''

''You might have considered all that when you concocted your little fable, my dear.'' He returned to his stance by the fireplace. ''Boredom is your problem. I shall not dance attendance on you, nor shall I expect any of the delightful tributes you propose.'' He fixed her with a cold stare. ''What I shall expect is behaviour fitting my station and the appearance of a match made voluntarily—and not simply for your convenience.''

''Your convenience as well, my lord!'' she shot back.

''Mine, too,'' he agreed with a nod. ''Now, we have been in here quite long enough, even for the door being partly open and even for an engaged couple. Are you ready to return and act your part convincingly?''

She tossed the broken fan into the fireplace. The expression she turned on her fiancé was sweet and bland as a child's. ''Of course, my lord. And there, too, you may make yourself known to my father.''

He paused with her at the door of the drawing rooms, consciously gathering stares, and murmured, ''My Christian name is Roger. Pray use it.''

''As you will, my lord.''

''Roger. Say it.''

''Roger,'' she echoed unwillingly.

''How endearingly it flows from your sweet lips,'' he remarked acidly. ''Come, let us greet my friend Lord Hulme.''

A tall, sun-bronzed, dark-haired gentleman in regimentals identical to Lord Rushden's, though without the Order of the Bath, hurried towards them with a wide smile on his face. ''Roger! Here you are! Anne is settled upstairs—'' He broke off, looking at Diana.

''Allow me to present my fiancée, the Lady Diana Bellrose,'' Roger said smoothly. ''My dear, this is my good friend, Michael, Viscount Hulme.''

''Entirely your servant, my lady.'' Lord Hulme smiled, carrying her hand to his lips while his eyes never left her face. She read surprise, admiration, and not a little amusement in his gaze, but could not help but like him for the friendly expression on his face.

"We have met," she replied smilingly. "At Almacks last year, I believe."

"Ah, I remember," he said and laughed. "I danced with you and stepped on your feet."

Diana turned to Lord Rushden with a cloying smile. "We have recently agreed not to tread on each other's toes, have we not, Roger?"

Lord Hulme gave a muffled cough. "Oh, dear," he murmured, turning from them.

"Has Anne been settled upstairs, Michael?" Lord Rushden asked his friend.

"Anne is here?" Diana asked eagerly.

"Yes, indeed. She did not feel equal to joining the company after the length of the journey from Midfield."

"It is to her, my dear," Lord Rushden added, "that I owe the happy news."

"Not her fault," Lord Hulme defended.

"Not at all." Lord Rushden gave him a killing look, which Diana did not understand. "I see your father over that way, my dear. Come, introduce me."

Lord Bellrose's expressions of delight were prodigious. Lord Rushden apologised for neglecting to sue formally for his daughter's hand, but pleaded some mysterious need for secrecy and Diana's forcible charms. Lady Diana smiled. Lord Bellrose welcomed the young man into the family. Lord Rushden bowed his thanks. Lady Diana smiled. Lord Bellrose asked when he could expect the happy day to occur. Lord Rushden deferred to Diana. Diana smiled.

She smiled through the rest of the evening. She smiled until her cheeks ached and her jaws were numb. The one note of grace in the whole hideous evening was that she knew the morrow would bring her a long coze with Anne—something she desperately needed.

When she finally returned home and reached the blessed solitude of her bedroom, she threw herself down fully dressed and attempted to indulge herself in tears of sheer nervous exhaustion. But her brain outfoxed her; she fell almost immediately asleep.

# — 10 —

THE NEXT WEEKS brought Roger every opportunity of observing his intended's talents, accomplishments, and charms. She showed him—or, rather, their acquaintance, for they were never alone—everything that was affable and delightful, and her high spirits and sprightly conversation were attributed to his happy return to town. Roger attended her at the Opera, at balls, at dinners, at musicales, at her residence, and at Sturbrough House, having thus every chance—which should have come before, not after, a betrothal—to learn her character. But not once did he speak with her alone.

He did not understand quite how this had been arranged, but he suspected it had much to do with his omnipresent sister. Diana and Anne were inseparable; where the one was found, the other surely was, and well within earshot, too. The incident of his giving Diana her ring was a case in point.

The day after the duchess's dinner and his first encounter with Diana, he and Michael went for an early-morning ride to Richmond Park and back. He had mentioned to Michael his intention of following through with all the proprieties of the engagement, which made his friend howl with laughter.

"I am quite serious," Roger said, offended. "I intend something in emeralds, or have you another opinion?"

"My opinion is that you've met your match, both literally and figuratively," Michael said with a grin. "Anne and I had fits imagining your encounter last night."

"You had best marry my sister and put her under your protection, before I find a really good excuse for murdering her." He rubbed his jaw, which still ached from Matilda's caress. "And speaking of sisters, your own has a right arm quite good enough to make her a candidate for the regimental boxing team.''

''God, how I wish I'd seen that,'' Michael said and sighed.

''To whose side are you loyal?'' Roger demanded.

''My own,'' was the laughing reply. ''Come, we'd best hurry. Lady Diana will be waiting for you.''

''And so shall Anne be waiting for you,'' Roger replied equably.

It proved to be so in the elegant breakfast parlour at Sturbrough House. Roger was greeted with a cool kiss from his sister and an even cooler nod from his fiancée. He and Michael filled their plates from the sideboard, and the four young people sat down to breakfast.

''You will be attending Lady Donald's musicale on Wednesday, naturally,'' Lady Diana began as Roger started in on eggs and sausage. ''And on Saturday night there is a card party at Lady Frewe's. Sunday mornings I am in the habit of going to church at ten, and you may ride home with me and take breakfast with us afterwards.''

Arrested in the act of bringing a forkful of eggs to his mouth, Roger stared at her across the damasked table. ''I beg your pardon?'' he asked blankly.

She turned the full force of her remarkable green eyes upon him. ''Come, my lord, we have no secrets from these our most intimate friends.'' She nodded at Michael and Anne, who both appeared totally engrossed in their meal, although Michael's shoulders shook suspiciously as he bent over his coffee cup. ''We shall all deal famously together, and have a wonderful laugh. Really, Roger, do look on the amusing side of things and try not to be stuffy.''

Two muffled choking sounds emitted from the other occupants of the room. Roger shot them furious glances, set his fork down, and leaned back in his chair with his breakfast untasted. ''I quite agree,'' he said slowly. ''The charade should be played with an eye to its entertainment value.''

''An excellent plan, my lord. Oh—you will grant me those words as a token of my affection for you, will you not? I must show proper respect for the lands and fortune and honours you bestow upon me with your hand, should I not?''

"I enjoin you to call me whatever you consider most natural and fitting," he responded, and resolutely applied himself to his cold eggs.

Anne and Michael being unwilling—or unable—to participate in the conversation, it was left to Roger and Diana to carry the burden of talk. And the first thing she spoke of was the ring.

"Do make it a diamond, Roger," she said. "I am excessively fond of diamonds."

"I had thought perhaps an emerald—"

"Oh, delightful!" She clapped her hands together and gave a charming smile that was so innocent he nearly missed the teasing glint in her eyes. "I haven't any emeralds! A diamond surrounded by emeralds—could there be anything more charming? Do you not think a ring like that would suit me perfectly, Anne?"

Miss Rushden gave a small squeak, her napkin pressed to her mouth. "Oh yes," she managed, and Michael started to cough.

"And pray do choose a large diamond, my lord. What is your opinion, Lord Hulme?"

"By all means," Michael said faintly, then got up to pour himself more coffee, still coughing and shaking.

"You see?" Diana applauded. "We are all agreed."

Roger observed his sister's watering eyes and his friend's quivering shoulders, and felt himself quite unequal to dealing with two hysterics and a cheerfully rapacious bride. He got to his feet. Then, in a moment of sheer inspiration, he plucked one of the roses from the vase on the table and extended it to Diana with a bow.

"Your laurels, my lady," he said sharply.

"I beg you do not rest upon them," Michael said from the sideboard, his voice sounding choked.

"Thorns!" Anne chirruped.

"Thank you, Roger," Diana said demurely. "I trust all our conversations will be this pleasant."

Roger took his leave. When he arrived half an hour later at his favourite jeweller's, he abandoned his planned speech about this being a present for a respectable female and ordered the largest diamond he could find. He picked out enough emeralds to surround it, and imagined the resulting horror with vicious glee.

After engaging in the round of activities proposed by her at that breakfast, Roger called for the ring at week's end, looking devilishly forward to presenting it to her. He was announced at an unfashionably early hour at the Bellrose residence, confident that his timing would provide him a private interview with Diana. But he had been outflanked; his fiancée sat in company with Anne and Michael, and all of them smiled most irritatingly as he bent over Diana's hand.

"You honour me with your early visit, my lord," she said with a pretty smile.

"Not at all," he protested, and sat down. His tailor had not cut his coat for the concealment of a jeweller's box; her eyes fastened upon the bulge in his pocket at once, and he cursed her silently.

"What is that?" she asked, pointing.

"A trifle," he said curtly.

"The ring," Michael announced gravely, his eyes sparkling.

They had entered into a conspiracy against him, Roger thought to himself, infuriated. Then, realising he had been outmanoeuvered, he reached into his own arsenal and found the proper attitude—a pose on one knee before Diana, seizing her left hand.

"Is this the correct picture of devotion?" he questioned sweetly.

She blinked in surprise, then, recovering with a quickness he could not help but admire, she pursed her lips and inspected him thoughtfully. "No, the other knee, I think."

The undignified action of switching knees almost set off his temper, but he accomplished it without a waver in his smile. "Better?"

"Admirable! Now, Roger—the ring?"

Every grievance against her was amply repaid as he watched her react to the size of the diamond and the surrounding emeralds. She fairly gulped; it was as big as his thumbnail and the emeralds were overpoweringly green. He let her contemplate it in its box for a moment, then took it out and slid it onto her finger. He got to his feet, dusted off his knees, and said, "I believe the proper words to be, 'I look eagerly to the day when you will make me the happiest of men,' or some such."

Diana gaped at the ring. It reached from knuckle to knuckle and glittered unmercifully. Roger grinned, gratified, and sat down next to her. "Well?" he prompted.

She swallowed again and glared at him. Then her expression smoothed into lash-fluttering appreciation. "It is exactly what I expected, my lord."

"I could do no less," he responded airily. "Ah, and here in this happy hour is your father." He rose and bowed. "I trust I may have your permission, my lord, to bestow a little trinket upon your daughter in commemoration of our joyous understanding?"

The episode had its amusements and satisfactions, especially in the eyes of Anne, Michael, and Lord Bellrose as they tried to ignore the size of the ring. But it might have been much more entertaining if he had been alone with Diana. Their encounters exhilarated him enough to make him wonder what she would be like without an audience.

This piquant desire to be alone with her for even five minutes increased over the weeks. For, despite the fulfillment of almost every one of her proposals for their charade—including the blushes upon his entrance—he came to the distinct and unhappy conclusion that he was for her exactly what she had said on the first night of their acquaintance: a convenience.

That he had said as much to her slipped his mind. That her behaviour was sanctioned and encouraged by him he conveniently forgot. That their engagement itself was entirely fictitious he managed to relegate to an area of his brain not often in use. He chafed, for he received all the benefits of a brilliant match, with all this carried with it of the approval of one's friends, the relief of one's relations, and the envy of one's world, but he enjoyed none of the privileges and private comforts that should have accompanied his situation.

That his mother was relieved was made abundantly clear in the six pages he received from her not three days after his arrival in London. His sisters Henrietta and Mary sent their congratulations, and Elizabeth, Caroline, and Catherine dispatched a gift of fresh Midfield roses to Diana along with their joint note of welcome into the family. Of all who knew of the engagement, only four knew the truth of it, and of those, three were in league against him—

especially in the matter of his spending a few minutes alone with his fiancée.

His chance came at last on a morning in which he had been expected to be on duty with his regiment. He was dismissed for the day and lost no time in riding to Sturbrough House, where he knew Diana, a constant visitor while his sister was there, would be sitting over coffee and the morning papers and post with Anne. To his surprise and delight, he found Diana quite alone in the library, seated at the desk, writing a letter.

"What luck to find you here!" he exclaimed, closing the door behind him and leaning back against it, grinning at her. Her expression told him precisely how pleased she was to encounter him thus, and he prepared to enjoy every moment of their skirmish. She was remarkably lovely in a pale peach ensemble, with white and gold ribbons threaded through her hair. It was not quite red, he thought, or auburn, but an interesting shade of russet that the sun touched with gold. Her startled green eyes soon regained their calm and tilted slightly up at the corners as she smiled at him.

"Such a happy surprise, my lord," she commented. "I have just finished the invitations to Anne's birthday party and was about to begin a letter."

"Pray return to your writing, my dear," he said as she closed the cover of a green leather writing pad.

"I find your company so much more entertaining than paper and pens," she responded sweetly. "To what do I owe the honour?"

"I am freed for the morning of my duties, and of course hastened to be with you. To whom were you writing?" He approached the desk and stood at her shoulder.

"Only a letter." She did not turn to look up at him, and he looked instead at the enormous diamond blazing from her left hand.

"Diana, Diana, you're not entering into the spirit of this at all! What you should have done, my dear, was to sit here modestly and listen with a blush as I complimented you on the evenness of your writing, the skill with which you form your letters, and the distinction of your capitals." He hitched one hip onto the desk and grinned down at her. "Shall we begin again?"

She flipped open the writing pad and scooted her chair back. "Look all you like," she said rudely.

He formed his reply, looking down at the writing, but unfortunately the first words out of his mouth were wholly spontaneous. "What could you possibly have to say to my mother?"

"I trust I know what my duties are," she replied tartly. "And what courtesies are due to your mother. Have you any objections to my thanking her for her kind note?"

"None at all," he answered, somewhat startled. He picked up the envelope, which already had many sheets of paper inside, and weighed it thoughtfully in his hand. "But surely it does not take all this to convey thanks."

Diana coloured deeply. "She asked me to provide her with a list of those persons I wish her to invite to the party she intends to give for us in July. It was kind of her to consult me."

"My mother is unfailing in matters such as these," he admitted, and set the letter down. "But I do not think I will be in London in July."

"You have had news from the War Ministry?" she asked eagerly.

He lifted his brows. "Are you so ready to be rid of me, then? True, I have somewhat hampered your little pleasures, but I trust that our association has not been too distressful to you? However, never fear, Diana—you will be spared my presence after very long."

"I only meant—" she began, and then her lips tightened. "You are the most odious man," she snapped. "To my simple request for information that may concern many of my friends, you reply in the most insulting terms. I shall indeed be happy to see you go."

"Then I shall certainly work to hasten the day," he said and bowed.

"Pray do—and make it a long absence."

"I am not likely to return from it," he said softly, and smiled with an unkind gleam in his eyes. "Has no one told you yet of the Rushden family?"

"Beyond the lands, titles, money, and thousand relations?"

"There is one other legacy to the name—an unconscionably early demise." He waved a hand negligently. "Not a single man of us has made it to his thirtieth birthday, I fear. So in any event, you are not to be long burdened with me, as I approach that age myself."

"Whatever are you talking about?"

"Has Anne not told you?"

"She has said nothing of the kind." Diana got to her feet and walked to the windows.

Roger sat in the chair she had vacated. "Pity; it would have saved my having to explain."

"It sounds perfectly absurd. Pray don't bother."

"But it is quite true. Here, I shall sketch the family for you." He pulled out a sheet of paper and sharpened a pen, and began to write. "Long ago I memorized their names and dates. You see, there is a certain morbid fascination in the list, at least for me. Come here, Diana, and see for yourself."

He wrote rapidly down the page, and at length she joined him, reading over his shoulder.

"Here's an interesting one," he said. "A very unfortunate Rushden indeed. The twelfth baron, who scarcely made it to age twenty. A good thing they married young in those days, for he left the thirteenth baron to carry on for him. We always seem to get sons on the first try. And here's the first Roger, who was six months old when he succeeded. There are more later on . . ." He continued writing, the names and dates flowing rapidly from his pen.

"This is absurd," Diana said again, but her voice wavered.

"Here is the sixteenth-century Roger, who died of some miserable fever or other. His son succumbed to the results of a duel at age twenty-six. But I am leaving out the most famous one—Henry, number seventeen, who was stung by a bee and died of it. He was twenty-four. Strange death, that, but in the line of duty—he was drilling a troop of horse at the time. Let me see . . . Ah, here's Great-great-great-great-grandfather Edward. He has the distinction of being the only Rushden to have had two wives—although both at the same time, and not successively! What a tangle that inheritance was! He got sons on both of them, and then died in some war or other. The exact battle escapes me." He came at last to himself. "And here we have number twenty-eight, your humble and obedient servant. I shall be thirty in January, my dear." He turned to look up at her with a malicious smile.

"Roger." She faltered, then went to the windows again. He wasted a moment admiring the curve of her shoulders and the slimness of her waist, then crumpled the paper in his hand.

"So you see you will not be bothered with me for very long. Be of good heart, my dear; I'm sure you'll catch another suitable husband."

"Oh, Roger, stop!"

"I must acquaint you with the facts. Indeed, I would have done so a week or more ago, had I not been certain my sister had already informed you."

She looked at him, frowning. "But—who will come after you? You have no son."

He pretended to be shocked. "Dare I venture to hope that you are offering to provide me with one?"

"Don't be disgusting!" she flared.

"I cry your pardon, my dear. I have everything arranged, you know. When Michael finally comes to his senses and marries Anne—and I see that you are cognisant of my sister's inclinations, as I am of Michael's—I have stipulated that their second son shall be the twenty-ninth baron. If they have no sons, or not enough, then I shall leave it to my other sisters to provide the heir. I should think they'll be reasonably prolific, and the odds are that among the six of them there will be an extra boy or two to do the honours. And since the direct male line will be broken, I should also think that the tradition will be broken as well. I am hoping so, at any rate, since I should hate to pass it along to a poor unsuspecting nephew."

Diana stared at him, aghast. Roger smiled acidly, getting to his feet.

"It was the need for an heir, you see, that made my mother so eager for my engagement and marriage. I must repeat that I am very grateful to you. I had no wooing to undergo, no false protestations of love to make. I am indebted to you for sparing me such nonsensical activities. I admit that I shall leave you with very little, but surely that rock upon your finger is a fair bride price?"

Diana went absolutely white. "I thank you for your kind consideration, my lord." She tugged at the huge ring and it came off her finger. "But after this insane recital I have concluded that my first opinion of you was the correct one, and no lady of decency would wish to be associated with you an instant longer than necessary!"

"Diana, do not you dare—"

But she had thrown the ring down at his feet. He stepped quickly to her and grasped her arm bruisingly.

"You are a fool if you think I will allow you to end our engagement now! Of what advantage is it? Why do you not wait until I am safely dead?"

"Roger! Let me go!"

"Not before you have put that ring back on, by God!" He bent, plucked the ring from the carpet, and held it our to her. "Wear it!"

"No!"

"It will be on your hand in five seconds or—put it back on, damn it!"

"No! You are the most odious—"

He wrapped one arm around her waist, crushing her to him. With the other hand he captured her left ring finger and forcibly returned the diamond to it. Then, just as she had ceased to struggle in his arms, he turned his head and his lips met the soft curling cloud of her hair. She had a light, clean, flowery scent, and she was a sweet armful of lovely young woman. Roger forgot himself. "Diana," he whispered, his lips buried in her hair.

She relaxed against him for an instant, and his grip became less fierce. He murmured her name again and tried to turn her face up so he could find her lips. But the inevitable of course occurred.

"Roger!"

Anne's voice, startled and appalled, from the open library door, broke them apart like a tree riven by lightning. Diana sprang from his arms like a frightened doe and raced from the room, and Roger was left to face his sister, whose eyes were round as saucers. He recovered enough of his aplomb to shrug.

"Lovers' quarrel," he said, trying to sound more composed than he felt. "I took perhaps a too-direct method of ending it. I trust you will make my excuses."

He walked past his silent, astonished sister, retrieved his hat, and sought Hulme Houses's familiar comforts, taking solace in Michael's study and a bottle of brandy.

# =11=

MICHAEL, WHO ARRIVED after luncheon but well before any other afternoon callers at the Sturbrough mansion, knew the moment he saw Anne that something was amiss. He accepted a glass of cordial and leaned back in his chair, listening to her polite but somewhat disjointed comments on the opera they had all attended several evenings before, and when she trailed off and stared at the rug, he finally asked her point-blank what the trouble was.

"I saw the most amazing thing this morning," she began reluctantly.

"Am I obliged to guess, or will you tell me?" he said with a smile.

"You could never guess anything near to it, so I will tell you. I saw Roger and Diana—in broad daylight—"

He raised his brows. "Shocking," he commented.

"Do not be so perverse," she snapped. "They were—he was kissing her!"

Michael began to laugh.

"I don't see what is so amusing," Anne said crossly.

"Did she resist?" he got out between paroxysms.

"Not that I could see. Michael, I have no idea what to think."

"Don't you?" He regained a modicum of calm. "Our Roger has tumbled head over heels. How fares Diana's opinion of him? Lower than ever?"

"That is just it. I cannot ask her, for she has locked herself in my room and will not open the door to me." Anne frowned and twisted the delicate chain of her bracelet.

"Is she crying?"

"Not that I could hear."

"Hmm." He set his glass down and crossed his long legs at the ankles, watching the play of sunlight over Anne's golden hair with the greatest of pleasure. "It has been my experience that ladies in love do a very great deal of crying."

"No doubt your experience is so vast upon the subject that we may safely acquit Diana of any such emotion," Anne observed frostily.

"There are certain exceptions."

"Pray do not enumerate them. I have been bored enough today by my Aunt Sturbrough's plans for my birthday party tomorrow night."

"For instance," he continued as if she had not spoken, "there are some young ladies who grow pale and thin when they are in love. Others flirt with every man in the world except the one to whom they are attached. And then there are the ones who deny they are in love at all and react with the greatest perversity when a gentleman attempts to express his admiration. Of which type are you, Anne?"

"I am not in love with anyone," she said briskly. "Your categorisation shall not include me, if you please."

He smiled to himself. "I see. What is your costume to be for the masquerade?"

"You know I will not tell you." She blinked, startled at the abrupt change in subject.

"Then how am I to know you?"

"I am sure you will find some method of discovering me."

"So I shall. Do you know, Annie, I have noticed a most peculiar response among ladies of wit and intelligence when they find themselves in love. Their impulse is always to sharpen those wits on the object of their affections."

"And do you know what I have observed?" she replied sweetly. "That a man who fancies himself enamoured of a lady invariably makes a complete fool of himself." She rearranged the folds of her dress. "Did you know that the guest list for my party has grown to four hundred?"

"I trust you were describing Roger."

"I do not know how we shall fit them all into the house."

"Or was there someone else in your mind?"

"Perhaps it will remain warm enough to dance on the terrace."

"I myself would be quite willing to make a fool of myself in a good cause."

Anne glared at him. "I recollect no time in our acquaintance when you have ever needed an excuse!"

Michael grinned. "Anne, will you marry me?"

"My costume is giving me a great deal of trouble," she said flatly, refusing to either address his question or look away from his direct gaze. "I cannot find the proper material for the veil."

"Miss Rushden, will you do me the very great honour of becoming my wife?"

"Someone from Chimene's is coming by later to show me samples."

"You will inform me, I trust, when I have made a big enough fool of myself to convince you of my sincerity?"

"I am worried that I might not find the right colour, though."

"Shall I go down on one knee, like Roger? He looked sufficiently ridiculous for even Diana's tastes, I should think."

"I hope I shall not have to send to everyone in town for the correct fabric."

"Anne, have you no fancy to become my viscountess?"

"Oh, damn you!" she finally exploded. "I told you years ago that you are the last man on earth I shall ever marry!"

"And so I shall be," he returned complacently. "The first and the last. Come, Anne, you know I love you."

"Oh, indeed?" she asked sardonically. "As much as you love Lady Olivia, or Miss Rickson, or Mademoiselle de Montal? Or any of the other score of ladies who have heard those words in the past?"

Stung, he waited a moment before answering very quietly, "I have never asked any woman to marry me, save you."

"I beg leave to doubt."

"I have never been more serious."

"And I have never believed you less."

Michael jumped to his feet, goaded. "What would you have of me? Passionate declarations in the moonlight? Or a ring as large and spiteful as the one Roger gave Diana? What would you have of me, Anne?"

She gazed up at him steadily. "Your heart."

"My—" He gaped at her. "Anne," he murmured at last. "It has always been yours, from the first time I saw you. I do not know what else to say."

"Yes."

"What?" He blinked.

"Yes," she said again, smiling up at him. "Or do you want me to cry?" Her eyes sparkled wickedly as she rose. "Shall I cry, or grow thin and pale? Would that convince you?"

"You mean you will?"

"Cry? Certainly not! I am far too happy for such nonsense!"

"No, not that," he said impatiently. "I mean, you will marry me?"

"I said as much, did I not? God help you, Michael, for I will indeed be your viscountess."

He searched her face with narrowed eyes. "This is no trick?"

She laughed and flung her arms round his neck. "How suspicious you are! Have I really mortified you all that much?"

Michael recovered his senses and his sense of humour. Trust his Anne to ruin what should have been a tenderly romantic scene. But he knew, gratefully, that brilliant sunlight suited her more than moonlit shadows, that laughter was infinitely preferable to tears, and that he wished nothing more than to be teased and tormented by her for the rest of his life. He took her shoulders and held her out from him as she linked her fingers behind his neck.

"You are a wretch," he announced. "Why should I not be suspicious of you? You will make my life one long misery with your plots and schemes." He grinned down at her. "Will your triumph be complete if I go down on one knee?"

"You are quite foolish enough without adopting so ridiculous a pose. And Michael, if you buy me a ring the size of Diana's, I shall refuse to see you ever again," she warned.

"Then I shall have to abduct you," he replied cheerfully. "Would you like to elope, Annie? I know you refused me once before, but it would save us all the bother of a wedding at St. Paul's. My father has been planning it this age."

"St. Paul's?" she echoed faintly.

"Of course. It is only fitting," he lectured with a wholly spurious gravity, "that the heir to the earldom be married with due pomp and ceremony. Our titles and dignities—"

"Michael!"

He began to laugh. "I am paying you back, my love, for making me wait so long."

She favoured him with a speculative gaze. "During which time you amused yourself quite adequately, or so I hear from Lady Olivia."

"Who?"

"Lady Olivia."

He grinned. "Who?"

Anne gave in with a laugh. "Very well. But *not* St. Paul's! Not even to please your father."

"What about pleasing me?" he complained.

"Oh, I believe I shall manage nicely enough," she murmured, and leaned up into his kiss.

Some minutes later, for the second time that day one young lady unintentionally interrupted the embraces of another. Diana's sudden and embarrassed appearance was greeted not with a fleeing lady and a humiliated gentleman, but with laughter and instant demands for her congratulations. When she comprehended what had just occurred, her expressions of joy and delight were everything Michael and Anne could have wished. They spent a happy hour together talking, teasing, and making outrageous plans for the wedding, which location was proposed for places ranging from Westminster Abbey to the muddiest field in East Anglia. Then Michael pleaded the necessity of writing to his father to advise him of his successful courtship—which Anne claimed was no courtship at all—and with more laughter and kisses Michael left them.

"I am perfectly happy," Diana told her friend, beaming. "Nothing in the world could possibly make me more so."

"Nothing?" Anne murmured, but then she smiled and added, "In truth, I am rather pleased with the day's work, myself."

"Pleased!" Diana crowed with laughter.

"Do you know, Di," Anne said in a more reflective mood, "I had set out this spring to accomplish just this—and then to refuse him."

"And found yourself instead to be in love." Diana nodded wisely. "It happens so, sometimes. Especially when one has the least expectation of it."

Anne searched Diana's eyes, but in them found no consciousness of Roger. She spared a sigh, then turned back to the happy topic. "Now it remains only to write to my mother, and to inform my aunt—oh, good God, Di, you don't think Michael will apply *en forme* to Roger for his permission, do you?"

"And Roger will refuse, of course, simply to watch Michael explode!"

"I shall murder the pair of them."

"No, you shall not. Viscountesses do not go about murdering people," Diana said severely, then spoiled the effect by giggling. "Will you announce the engagement at your birthday ball?"

"I shall wait and see what Michael says," Anne replied demurely.

Diana stared and begged to know if Anne felt quite well. "For," she concluded, "I have never known you so compliant."

"Did you not say it? I am to be a model of dignity and the pattern of propriety now I am to be a viscountess." Then she, too, giggled.

"That is the Annie I know," Diana said with some relief. At this moment, her carriage was announced and the two young ladies walked to the door of the room. "Anne—I am sorry for my lurid behaviour today—"

"Shall I enjoin my brother to absent himself from the ball?"

"No!"

Anne grinned. "And that is the Diana I know," she concluded triumphantly. "I have it on good authority that Roger is to be dressed as a perfectly villainous corsair."

"He should fit the role admirably," Diana replied, a little grimly, and took her leave.

Diana's own costume for Anne's *bal en masque* would cause a sensation, and she had planned it with precisely that intent. She had rejected the usual milkmaid or Queen Elizabeth costumes, of which there were bound to be dozens, and abandoned as well any thought of using her grandmother's finery, which reposed in decaying splendour in the attic trunks. She had taken as her theme the dress of a troupe of gypsies she had glimpsed a few years earlier on a drive through the Kentish countryside. With a few alterations in deference to modesty, and allowing for the more luxurious materials available to her and the imperfections of memory, she had designed a unique ensemble. The skirt was of moss-green velvet trimmed extravagantly around the hem with gold embroidery. Above it she had chosen a white silk blouse open at the throat and a black velvet corselet laced tightly to her figure. The lavish decoration on the skirt was repeated on the corselet and even on the stiff taffeta petticoat that made the skirt bell out from her waist and swish with a most luxurious sound. A necklace of gold coins went around her throat and a similar chain was looped around her head with a green veil, glistening with gold thread, attached to it to imperfectly cover her long, unbound hair.

There was nothing Diana loved better than a masquerade, and since the happy news of Anne and Michael's engagement was to be formally announced there, she had a double reason to look forward to the evening. Any lingering unease she felt after her contretemps with Roger had disappeared rapidly; the more she considered his impulsive embrace, the more smugly she anticipated seeing him again. His "any young lady would have done" gave her ample cause to grin, for he had proved he was not so immune to her as he claimed.

She rested through most of the day, staying indoors and taking her meals in her rooms. It took her two hours to dress, and by the time she had placed the black domino mask over her face and stood in front of the mirror to survey the effect of her costume, she was in a pleasurable fever of anticipation. On impulse she whirled around on her bare toes, skirts flying, gold coins jingling from neck, wrists, and ears. Removing one of the bracelets, she fastened it around her ankle and kicked the leg high, winning a scandalised gasp from her maid. Let Roger think she would do as well as any other young lady—let him think so, if he could.

Her shoes waited for her on the chair, little velvet slippers decorated in gold, but she capriciously decided to go without them. The evening was warm, and stockings and shoes would not be in the character of a gypsy dancer. Shaking her head again to hear the coins tinkle, she snatched up a fringed black shawl and ran lightly downstairs to her waiting, impatient parent.

Lord Bellrose had spent the day with the family solicitor, working out the details of the financial proposals to be made to Lord Rushden regarding the marriage. Diana listened with half an ear, murmuring, "Yes, Papa," and "How interesting, Papa," at what she assumed to be correct intervals. Her father went on at great and boring length, and it was not until they were almost at the Sturbrough mansion that Diana finally heard an important piece of news.

"Your cousin Charles has kindly agreed to act as our agent in this."

"Charles?" She turned to her father, interested at last. "He is back, then?"

"Has been this se'ennight. Stopped in at The Mill to see how things were." The Mill was the Bellrose country estate in Hampshire. "Brought back all sorts of nonsense for me to read, but useful, now you're negotiating this marriage."

"He has not been to see me," Diana complained. For many months last winter Charles had paid her attentive and amusing court; he had been one of the "young bucks" about whom her father had grumbled prior to the "engagement" to Lord Rushden. She recalled that after the news was generally known, he had left London. In the difficulties that had followed, she had forgotten all about him, but now, as she reflected back, his sudden absence was rather flattering. And his neglect puzzled her.

"We can trust him to look after your interests," Lord Bellrose went on complacently. "I'm no hand at that kind of thing. We'll get a proper settlement out of Rushden, no doubt. With all those sisters to marry off, his fortune's not limitless and his man will want quite a bit from us." He snorted, then chuckled. "Charles will see it right, Di, never fear of that."

"It seems somewhat—vulgar," she ventured.

"Nonsense. Why, when your mother and I were married, it took eight months to work out the provisions. You'll have everything of mine and hers, of course, but we'll tie it all up for your children. With the Rushden and Bellrose names, and The Mill and the house here, plus all that land—" He chuckled again. "Your girls will be able to pick and choose as they please! What d'you say to that, eh?''

"How interesting," she said, concealing her distaste. Then that emotion was lost as she recalled Roger's mocking little history of his family, and for the first time she realised how much bitterness had been in his voice. Rejecting the odd little stirring in her heart, she arranged her face and her thoughts into smiles and took her father's hand to descend from the carriage and up the steps of Sturbrough House.

As she had anticipated, the place was full of peasant girls and Elizabeths. Here and there as well were medieval couples, a Red Indian whose feathers wilted from his leather headband, several pirates, Arthurs and Guineveres galore, and a few fanciful creations that belonged to no period at all. Kitty Kirby, unmistakable even in her extravagantly pearled costume as a sea princess, walked by on Young George's arm. Diana was hard put not to laugh aloud; Young George had elected to complement his sugarplum's costume by coming as Neptune, and was not yet skilled in the safe handling of a trident almost as tall as he.

Diana saw her father happily talking with his friends, and went at once to the ballroom. She was partnered immediately, and as the heat and crush grew, was glad she had chosen so light a silk for her blouse. The atmosphere grew breathless as the dancers warmed with exercise and the thousand candles contributed to the temperature. The ballroom was festooned in gold and silver cloth accented with green, and the motif of Tudor roses was everywhere. The roses themselves, scores of them in a hundred vases and woven about the columns, were fast wilting in the heat. But some kind person had had the goodness to open the terrace doors and soon the assembly revived, although the roses were early casualties.

Diana, sipping on a welcome glass of champagne brought her by a gentleman dressed as King Charles II, began to wonder when Anne and Michael would make their entrance. The duchess, seated on a small dais and to whom Diana had made her obeisances upon her arrival, could be seen to glance with a frown toward the staircase from time to time. Diana excused herself from the replica Stuart king, whose long black wig was askew, and moved toward the duchess.

At that precise moment someone tapped her lightly on the wrist. She turned and beheld a man of middling height, well set up, wearing to excellent advantage a costume corresponding to the popular notion of an Arabic prince. His dark complexion and black eyes were in perfect keeping with his selection of a flowing white robe, bound in at the waist with multicoloured cords twisted about each other. He smiled at her, touched his forehead and then his breast, and moved away.

"Charles!" she began, but a hush suddenly enveloped the company and the music stopped. Diana turned, forgetting about her cousin—for Charles it had surely been—and smiled. Descending the stairs were Michael and Anne.

# ===12===

THERE CAN BE few events more satisfying for a couple than their entrance into a ballroom where all festivities are in honour of their own happiness. The pair stood at the top of the steps, making the most of their moment, and the four hundred assembled to wish them well were nearly unanimous in their smiles. Only a few people noticed that the enthusiasm of a few ladies of Michael's acquaintance was a trifle impaired.

The theme of their costumes was the same: she was in white, he in crimson, representing Elizabeth of York and Henry Tudor. The requisite cap was a little off kilter on Michael's riot of curls, and Anne would have difficulty keeping him from treading on her dress's train, but the choice was most appropriate and the significance understood by almost everyone. The Boyden-Hulmes were descended (irregularly, to be sure) from the Lancastrians, and the Rushdens numbered among their ancestors (equally irregularly) connexions to the Yorkists. Anne's necklace of pearls had been in her family for several centuries and was said to have belonged to Queen Elizabeth herself; the bejewelled chain Michael wore about his wide shoulders had been dug at the last minute out of the Boyden-Hulme collection, and he carried it with a panache that belied his reluctance at wearing it.

"It's slipping," she whispered to him as they started down the stairs.

"Damn," he muttered, shifting his shoulders to adjust it.

"The exquisite Lady Olivia is not here," Anne observed in a low voice as they made their progress. "How cowardly of her."

"I thought you were to cease plaguing me about women who no

longer exist." Michael bowed to the duchess.

"I agreed to marry you, Michael, not to become a saint."

He turned to her with a grin. "Sainthood is the very last thing I have in mind for you, Annie. So many of them were virgin martyrs."

Sweetly she answered, "And when, pray, shall I have the opportunity of disqualifying myself?"

"Anne!"

She laughed at him, and they were swept up in a tide of congratulations. Only by slipping an arm around his betrothed's waist did Michael succeed in staying at her side. The crush at last abated and the dancing began anew, affording them the chance to appreciate at leisure the site of the ball.

"I managed to dissuade the duchess from some of her ideas," Roger said from behind them. They turned, he kissed Anne's cheek, and he went on. "For instance, the arms of both our houses, done eight feet high and suspended from the ceiling by gold and silver chains."

Michael shuddered.

"Although I was rather sorry that Anne persuaded her from the use of cooing lovebirds over the doorways." Roger grinned. "The argument being, of course, that the poor birds might catch cold in a draught."

"Anne never said that," countered Michael. "More likely she pointed out that our guests might find themselves . . . gifted from above, shall we say? . . . upon entering and leaving the—"

"Michael! If you insist upon being coarse, I shall never speak to you again."

"Splendid!" he agreed at once. "I have always considered silence to be the most admirable quality in a wife." He squeezed her waist, laughing.

"I see Michael opened the family vault for you, Annie," Roger observed, glancing pointedly at her left hand. The ring upon it was a diamond set in silver, and emphatically nowhere near as large as Diana's.

"They suit her better than Matty," Michael began, but happened to look around. His eyes went wide. "Ah," he murmured irrepressibly. "The future Lady Rushden."

"Di!" Anne exclaimed. "I should have known you anywhere. Do take off your mask so we may talk comfortably. I can never bear conversing with a mask."

"This cannot be Lady Diana," Roger announced. The three others stared at him as he went on blandly. "My fiancée would never so forget herself and her position as to come barefoot to a ball." He bowed over the ring he himself had bestowed upon her and finished loudly. "I am certain I see her over there, beside the duchess. Pray excuse me." And he walked off.

The cheeks below the black domino mask turned crimson and then white, green eyes flashing with anger. Michael spent a moment admiring the results of Roger's devilment, then murmured an apology and swept Anne off to dance.

"Is she really barefoot?" he whispered as they took their place in the set.

"Oh, hush! You are as despicable as Roger!"

"I merely asked—"

"Michael, you are not to plague her," she told him severely. "If he makes her a scene tonight I shall roast him! And whatever possessed him to come in that outlandish attire? What on earth has he got on?"

Michael glanced over her shoulder at the tall figure of his friend and shrugged. "Damned if I know. Probably something he dug up from a friend in the regiment. Smile at me, my love—or I shall try to remember Lady Olivia."

Roger had, in fact, expended just as much time and thought on his costume as Diana had, and the puzzlement of his sister and friend would have annoyed him. He considered his presentation of a Cossack horseman to be quite spectacular with its wide trousers gathered into tall black boots, the brilliant blue shirt embroidered in multicoloured silk and tied with a huge satin sash. The sleeves were a trifle cumbersome, and he was not yet used to the buttons that marched up the side of the shirt to the high collar, but he thought himself a dashing figure and certainly most original. A young colonel of the Czar's armies had visited England several years earlier, and after a week's competition in riding, shooting, and drinking had shown the young Russian that not all Englishmen were foppish prigs, he had returned to his homeland with a favourable report. He had sent back to England a present of a magnificent stallion and the Cossack regalia as a tribute to Roger's horsemanship—and to show his appreciation for the dozen cases of Madeira Roger had sent him from Midfield's cellar. The stallion had proved himself at stud, but the Cossack clothes had never been worn until tonight.

He danced exclusively with his cousins before supper, and then partnered any young lady who happened to take his fancy. He did not once seek out the beautiful "gypsy" girl, although he quite often saw the swirl of her green skirt as she spun past him. This sight did not materially improve his temper, and the observation that quite often she seemed to be in the arms of an Arabian prince and enjoying their dances far too much had no happy effect either. By the midnight unmasking he contrived to be next to Diana so as to monopolise her from then on.

When her mask was removed he apologised profusely for not having recognised her earlier, his protestations being everything that was charming and insincere. She suffered them with a cool smile, then excused herself as being promised to one of his cousins for the waltz. Roger looked down at the hapless young man who was attending his very first great ball.

"I am sure you will indulge me, Percy," Roger said quellingly.

"Of—of course, Roger," Percy stammered, and fled his cousin's formidable frown.

"You are disgusting. I have no intention of dancing with you!" Diana turned away.

"Nor have I any intention of dancing with you. Come with me."

"No!"

He ignored her protest and, trusting with perfect faith that her breeding would not allow her to make a scene in the ballroom, steered her firmly out the doors, down the steps, and onto the gravelled path.

"Ouch!"

"Oh, I forgot. No shoes." He bent and swept her up into his arms.

"Roger!"

"I beg you will not shriek in my ear, Diana."

"Put me down!"

"When we are safely private," he answered, glad that she was not so foolish as to wriggle. He walked on, carrying her easily but with little gentleness, until they were around a bend in the path and out of sight and earshot of the terrace. Then he deposited her with scant ceremony on a bench. Gazing sourly down at her furious face, her green eyes fiery in the uncertain moonlight, he began abruptly. "If you still wish to return that ring and call it quits with me, I shall not deter you."

Diana gasped.

"This farce has gone on long enough," he went on, clasping his hands behind his back. "You do not wish its continuance any more than I, as your actions of yesterday morning showed most plainly. I have been thinking it over, Diana, and I have decided to give you leave to break off the engagement. Any date in the near future will be satisfactory."

"*Give me leave*—?" she repeated in a strangled voice.

"Yes. It will save you the trouble of mourning me, after all." He paced several steps away. "And think of the cachet when news of my demise comes—the inference will of course be that I was careless because of my despondency over losing you. Unable to face a life without you, and so forth. You must admit, it has a nice romantic brio about it."

He glanced over his shoulder to see how she was taking this. Her eyes were enormous, her face ash white, her hands clenched together on the folds of her skirt. He waited for her to say something, then shrugged.

"It will be for the best, you must admit. I—"

"You are the most loathsome man I have ever known!" Diana leapt to her feet, careless of the stones covering the path. "Give me leave to end the engagement, indeed! Save me the trouble of mourning you! Romantic brio be damned, my Lord Rushden!" she spat. "After insulting me in every possible fashion, including this hideous vulgar ring, not to mention your repulsive conduct of yesterday, you now decide you have had your fun? You wish to be rid of me? Not bloody likely, my lord!'' She planted both feet and rested her fists on her hips. ''Mine you are and mine you stay until *I* decide to have done with you!''

Roger heard this with increasing outrage, offset by the uncomfortable desire to take this flaming fury into his arms again. The dichotomy of emotions rendered him effectively speechless.

''And as for that idiocy about a cachet! If you are determined to get yourself killed, then pray do not place the blame for it upon me! My hero!''

''That is enough! I will hear no more of—''

''You will hear whatever I care to say, and you may like it or loathe it. It matters not to me!''

''Diana, I absolutely forbid—''

''Forbid what?'' she said with a sneer, standing her ground. He advanced on her. She glared up at him, unmoving. ''Go on, off to Portugal or India or the bloody Antipodes if you like! You are just as like to die of one war as another. Just which one makes no difference to you, I'm sure! Just as which lady makes no difference as chief mourner at your funeral! I swear to you, Roger, if you get yourself shot, I will—''

She bit her lower lip; he caught his breath. ''You shall what?'' he asked in a soft, cold voice.

''I shall—oh damn you to hell!'' she shouted and, picking up her skirts to show him a fascinating view of slim ankles and exquisite legs, ran off into the darkness.

''Diana!''

But he came to a halt after only a few steps, knowing pursuit would be useless. He turned and went disconsolately back to the house, worrying, absurdly, about the coarse gravel and her unshod feet.

# =13=

ROGER WAS SPARED any further debacles by the demands of his sister's wedding. Henrietta married her country gentleman a week after Anne's birthday ball, in a simple ceremony at Midfield's parish church. Diana wrote a pretty note to Lady Rushden begging to be forgiven for not attending and pleading the sudden, severe summer cold that had overtaken her.

"Brought on, doubtless, by her madness in running about barefoot," Roger commented sourly to Michael in private after learning the gist of the letter. But Michael was profoundly uninterested in Roger's problems with Diana; he was far too busy with Anne, and considered Henrietta's wedding no more than a dress rehearsal for his own.

The rest of the family demonstrated equal lack of attention. Weddings were most definitely in the air, Henrietta's being the most immediate, Mary's to come in a few weeks, and Anne's to plan for the winter. Lady Rushden, who normally would have been primarily involved with Roger's plans in the same direction, thought of her son scarcely at all. When she did think of him, it was with a heartfelt sigh of relief that his nuptials would be overseen by Diana's family and not herself. All her ladyship would be required to do at her son's wedding would be to look elegant, and cry.

She received ample opportunity to practise her tears, for Henrietta's wedding seemed beset by every difficulty. Three days of solid rain turned the roads into sticky mires and every pathway into a river of mud. Roger forgot to bring his dress uniform down from London, and the groom dispatched to fetch it, having no idea which was the desired item, brought down the entirety of his wardrobe. The bridegroom, suffering an agony of nerves, arrived at the church a full day in advance of the ceremony and only the vicar's strongest persuasions and best port convinced him that his intended had not jilted him. Henrietta's dress came late from London, and it was discovered the measurements had been mistaken, so that the night before the wedding was spent in frantic sewing. An army of relatives descended upon Midfield to be suitably housed and entertained, and the various family factions had to be kept at peace for the duration. Most mothers-of-the-bride would, by the morning of the wedding, have given way to strong hysterics; Lady Rushden was unique in her self-possession.

But only until the knot was tied; she then wept copiously with joy and sheer relief when, with the sun shining bravely outside, her eldest daughter became Mrs. John Beaupre, mistress of Troquey Manor, six thousand acres, and ten thousand pounds per annum.

The moment the wedding party set foot back in Midfield, the rain began again in earnest. This had little bearing on the festivities or on the departure at dusk of the bride and groom for his house a mere five miles away. But when the next morning showed the clouds still thick and black and likely to remain so, many of the guests chose to stay on rather than brave the roads. These crowded conditions—for though the house could pack in close to seventy guests in reasonable comfort, on the second night they sat down eighty-six to dinner—were as wearing on Lady Rushden's nerves as the preparations for the wedding had been. Not even the condition of the roads, therefore, kept her from her plan of removing to Bath to recuperate from her labours and refresh herself for the coming trials of Mary's wedding. She set out four days after Henrietta's celebrations, with Mary, Elizabeth, and Caroline attending her.

The next day a second party set out, consisting of Michael, Anne, and Catherine, bound for Chetley Castle. The visit had been arranged so that the earl might come to know his future daughter-by-marriage more fully, and as little as Anne relished the attentions of the countess and Lady Matilda, she felt that the sooner she learned how best to live with them, the better.

Roger stayed long enough to see the last of his guests gratefully gone—for, with all the capriciousness of early summer, the sun had glowed golden to dry the roads to passability within eight days—and then set about enjoying his home in unaccustomed silence and privacy. He rode every decent horse in his stables, fished in his river, attended to estate business, read books he had not suspected were in his libraries, reviewed his wine cellar and picture collection, and took long walks that afforded him enchanting vistas of his acres and woods. And within a fortnight of his family's departure, he was bored to distraction. Midfield, much as he loved it, was insupportable without the presence of his mother and sisters. In whatever manner he filled up his days, there still came, each evening, that awful hour when he sat at the vast table in the dining salon alone.

For boredom and loneliness there were always remedies. So he ordered his packing and went back to London. There were any number of friends and relatives with whom he might have stayed for a time in rural splendour, but he sought the brilliance of the capital as the antidote to his miseries. The fact that he had every expectation of seeing Diana in London did not enter his head; he simply could not get her out of it. He would not have admitted to himself, even had it occurred to him, that he missed her, and in fact told himself at least five times a day that he did not think of her at all. Yet on the morning of his arrival back in town he presented himself at the Bellrose residence.

He was faced with a startled under-footman who bowed and begged to inform his lordship that Lord Bellrose and her young ladyship had gone to the country to speed her ladyship's recovery from her illness.

Roger was at a total loss. Diana could be anywhere from Cornwall to Yorkshire, for all he knew. He could not apply to her friends for her direction, since it was to be assumed that a lady would inform her fiancé of her whereabouts. Neither could he ask the footman, for servants' gossip travelled even more swiftly than that of their employers. Wherever and however he enquired, it would be around London in a matter of hours that he had no idea where his own betrothed was to be found.

Infuriated, bereft of companions, bored, and feeling all the idiocy of his position, Roger took refuge in a course of action that had served him tolerably well in the past. He appropriated a suite of rooms in an hotel on a block owned by his family, and gave a party that lasted for three days.

His aunt, the duchess of Sturbrough, heard of the revels on their second scandalous night. Her butler, who was cousin to Roger's valet, begged leave to tell Her Grace that his lordship was in a fair way to drowning himself as well as his sorrows in Irish whiskey, and could Her Grace be prevailed upon to end this riot? Her Grace responded by waiting another full day for the liquor to further incapacitate her nephew before she sent him a note commanding him to wait upon her. Since it had been thirty years since any of the duchess's relations had dared disobey her edicts, on the morning of the fourth day Roger presented himself in Her Grace's drawing room.

The duchess was the eldest of the three marvellously beautiful Misses Blackhearst. The youngest, Roger's mother, had captured the Rushden name and fortune; the middle sister had snared an earl; and the eldest, Margaret, had won the duke of Sturbrough. Their Graces had not been blessed with sons, so all of her six nephews, Roger in particular, were visited with every attention she would have afflicted on male progeny of her own. Older than Lady Rushden by twenty years, she yet retained the fine bones and brilliant blue eyes that had made all three sisters famous, and her skin, even at sixty-seven, was a miracle. She knew everyone worth knowing and had received proposals, honourable and otherwise, from every male of her generation. It had been her influence with an old suitor, now highly placed in the War Ministry, that had ended Roger's exile, and now she proposed using the same source to put a stop to her nephew's disgraceful conduct by giving him something useful to do.

Roger approached her and bowed low—an activity most ill advised, as it made his head spin. His aunt eyed him with a cold, singularly shrewd gaze, enquired acidly after his health, and requested information on the exact number of bottles it took to forget Lady Diana Bellrose.

A blistering hour later Roger was back in his rooms, and in a more physically comfortable state. His mental agitation had not been materially assisted, however, by the hot bath, large breakfast, and soothing potions administered to him by his valet. Having had the truth of his feelings borne home to him by the duchess, he reviewed his every word and action regarding Diana and hers regarding him, and found a catalogue of fury, insults, and ill usage that should have had him ready to wring her lovely neck. Yet revenge upon her was the last thing on his mind. Forget her? Impossible. His brain reeled at the shock of his feelings.

It should not be taken as a definitive comment on Roger's constancy, however, to say that when he received a message in the early afternoon to attend a very important meeting at certain offices, all thought of Diana fled his mind. Further, the fact that in the next two busy days she crossed his mind only in bittersweet glimpses must not be viewed as a lack of sincere attachment or a reversal of his emotions. For Roger was first and foremost a soldier, like all his breed, and the command to serve King and country was naturally met with all the powers of heart and head that he possessed.

He wrote to his mother to inform her he would not have the pleasure of waiting on her at Bath and escorting her back to Midfield for Mary's wedding, as he had planned. He then dispatched an express to Chetley Castle and began to pack.

Receipt of Roger's missive was delayed a few hours by Michael's having gone with Anne on a long, rambling ride around the estates that one day would be theirs. They had spent a great deal of time doing so, since it had the double advantage of allowing them solitude and getting them away from the importunities of the countess and Lady Matilda. They laughed together over something Catherine had reported to Anne that morning, to the effect that the countess thought that the pair were surveying their possessions before the old earl was even dead. Lady Matilda had seconded the notion with the observation that Chetley must certainly be far more than Anne could ever have hoped to gain, and of course it was far better and larger than Midfield and the other Rushden possessions.

"Sour grapes," Michael said with a laugh. "Will she ever recover/ from the loss of your brother?" he sang in her ear.

"It appears the whole world has lost Roger. No one has heard from him in weeks." Anne frowned.

But they both recognised the handwriting on the letter presented to Michael upon their return to the castle. He ripped it open, dismissed the tired courier, and scanned the lines. Held it out to Anne.

"Read it," he said, and turned away to inspect the huge bouquet of roses on the hall table.

"'Michael,'" Anne read aloud, "'Kiss Anne good-bye and come to town instantly. My duty to your father and the countess. Rushden.'" She frowned before reading the postscript. "'Instantly, you idiot!'" She looked at Michael in alarm. "Instantly! He cannot mean—"

Michael looked at her reflexion in the mirror above the roses. In her green riding habit and hat, a gossamer veil streaming down her back, she had never been more beautiful. "He does," he said shortly, and started down the hall. "Be a darling and order my things packed, Anne. I must go to my father."

He left her in the hallway grappling with this foretaste of life with a soldier, and proceeded to his father's study.

"I am directed by Roger to leave for London at once," he told the earl without preamble.

Sharp blue eyes raked him, and the older man nodded. "Good."

"I depend upon you to see Anne and her sister safe home to Midfield," Michael went on.

"Of course." The earl got to his feet and hobbled to where his son stood at the bookcases. "I like her, Michael. She'll do you very well."

"I am honoured that you think so, my lord." Michael gave him a tender, wistful little smile that reminded him forcibly of his late wife. For once his habitual roar was muted as he addressed his only son.

"I wish she would consent to stay with us here for a time, but I daresay her mother will want her at Midfield, what with this wedding and Roger gone to Portugal with you."

"Yes." Michael went to retrieve his father's cane. Handing it to him, their eyes met. Michael hesitated a moment, then said, "I shall be packed and gone within the hour."

"I shall charge myself with making your excuses to Lady Chetley and Matilda."

"Thank you."

"Michael . . ." He spoke to the shelves of books. "I hope I can trust you not to disappoint Anne."

Michael rightly took this to mean he was not to get himself killed and break not only Anne's heart but also his father's. Glancing up at the portrait of his mother over the fireplace, it dawned on him for the first time that he might not see it, or his father, or Anne ever again. Breathing suddenly became difficult. Always before his marching orders had brought him nothing but a sense of excitement and high adventure. But he had Anne now, a most compelling reason to stay in England. And his father, though he had looked stronger these last weeks, was growing old. Michael gazed for a moment at the lined face, the silvered hair, the firm uncompromising lips, and the eyes that were anywhere but on him.

The moment passed, and Michael took refuge in his usual wry grin. "I shall direct my energies to winning plenty of medals so that she need not blush for my heroism."

His father snorted. "Too many and you'll drown out the music at the wedding, jingling most vulgarly down the aisle. Just see to it you comprehend the ineligibility of a bridegroom who does not show up for the wedding, boy. And here is Wanson, who needs to know countless things about your departure, I trust," he added as the butler edged into the room. "You need not see me before you go, Michael." He limped painfully back to his desk and sat down, pulling out an account book and picking up his pen.

Michael watched him for a few seconds, then looked once more at the portrait of his mother. Then he turned on his heel and left the room.

He paused in the upper hallway long enough to order his horse saddled and a fresh one made ready for the courier, and was pleasantly surprised to find that Anne had already taken care of it for him. Her efficiency extended to informing the cook that his young lordship required a light dinner upon the instant and a well-provided packet of food for his journey. Wanson informed him of all this, and then asked to know if he preferred cold chicken or cold ham. But the warm glow of Anne's care faded rapidly when he entered his rooms to find her calmly and efficiently packing his valise under the disapproving eye of the head footman.

"That will be all, Robert," Michael said sharply. The footman bowed and absented himself, careful to leave the door open in deference to Miss Rushden's reputation.

Miss Rushden's fiancé slammed the door shut and rounded on her with a furious glare. "What d'you think you're doing?" he demanded.

"Packing," she replied succinctly, and folded another shirt.

"I can see that! Of all the improper—"

"Oh, really, Michael." She sighed patiently, reaching for a pile of clean linens. "Don't be so gothick. We are engaged, after all. And it was you yourself who closed the door."

"That's nothing to the point," he fumed, angry and not quite knowing why. He snatched up a stack of folded stockings. "It isn't proper for you to be rummaging about in my underwear!"

"Your dinner should be up directly," she went on, seemingly oblivious to his comment or his emotion. "I hope the countess will not mind, but I asked Wanson to feed that poor young man who brought Roger's note."

On cue, a knock sounded at the door and Robert came in with a tray. Michael waved him to a corner table. When they were alone again, Anne arranged the table next to the bed and told Michael to eat before the soup got cold. Then she went back to packing.

As he watched her, his anger evaporated. And although he had had no lunch and it was past time for something to eat, his appetite vanished as well. The sunlight tangled in her golden hair limned the fineness of her profile and shadowed her neck and shoulders, accented the delicate poise of her head. His heart turned over.

"Anne," he whispered, and put the table aside.

"Do you think there is room for another shirt?"

"Leave the shirts," he said, holding out his hands.

"You will remember your cloak, Michael? I do not like to think of you riding all night in the chill."

"Anne . . ."

"And you will remember that summers are very hot in Portugal?

111

Do not forget that the sun is not so gentle there.''

"How did you know it was Portugal?''

She looked up from the valise. "Roger loves me, and he would not interrupt my happiness for any other reason than that you are to leave, very quickly. The logical destination is Portugal, and it may be—it will be a long time—'' She faltered.

He opened his arms to her and she fell into them. Only a few moments later Robert knocked at the door again to inform his lordship that the horses were ready.

"Go away!'' Michael called, lifting his face for only an instant from the tumble of Anne's disordered hair.

"Beg pardon, my lord, but—''

"It is all right, Robert,'' Anne said, drawing away from Michael. "His lordship will be down at once.''

"Anne—'' He tried to pull her close again, but she wriggled away and went to close and lock his valise.

"Come in, Robert,'' she said serenely, holding out the bag and smiling at the young man. Michael could not help a grin at the picture she presented: the soul of propriety but for the sunny cascade of her hair and the tears wet on her cheeks.

"Very good, my lady.'' Robert bowed, took the valise, and left without a flicker of expression.

"Come, Michael,'' Anne said firmly, "you cannot intend to waste all this efficiency by keeping your horses waiting.''

He held out his hands again. "Help me up.''

"What, too feeble to rise on your own?'' she teased, but went to him and took his fingers in her own. He gripped tightly and would have pulled her down into his arms again. She surprised him by leaning backward and pulling with astonishing strength. He was on his feet before he knew it, but the process of catching his balance served his purpose, for the momentum carried him forward and he seized her in his arms.

"There is one of Roger's instructions I have not yet followed,'' he murmured. And, forestalling any questions, protests, or comments, he captured her mouth with his own.

A few minutes later someone rapped on the door frame again. It interrupted them only long enough to draw breath, for Anne had lost all inclination to leave his arms, just as he had lost all thought of leaving her. Yet after only a moment more Michael let her go of his own accord, his breathing very unsteady.

"I'll leave now," he said huskily, snatching up his cloak from a chair. "Or Roger will have a very good reason to call me out."

Anne's eyes held a frank invitation to stay. Michael trembled for an instant, but shook his head and resorted to his old rueful grin.

"What would you like me to bring you, Annie? A shawl? Pearls? Combs like a Spanish dancer?"

She made an heroic effort and recovered herself, and he blessed her for her understanding. "Bring me no gifts, or I shall suspect you of trying to ease your guilt. A man only brings presents when he has been flirting with other ladies, and I am told the women in Portugal are dark-eyed beauties."

"You are unfailingly cruel," he protested.

Again the knock sounded at the door, more urgent this time, and Robert's voice called, "My lord!" Anne flung an anguished glance to the door, then at Michael, and bit her lip.

"Oh, Michael—come home to me safely, please—"

He said nothing, but took her hands and pressed a kiss into each palm. Then, fearing that to stay any longer would mean never to leave, he turned and strode out of the room.

# 14

"DI, YOU SIMPLY must stop this moping. It is doing you very real damage." Anne frowned worriedly at her friend as they sat in the shade of an ancient elm in the Bellrose gardens, Anne with her needlework and Diana with a book whose pages she had not turned in over an hour.

"I'm sorry." Diana smiled wanly. "I'm a miserable companion. You would have done better to stay with Lady Matilda and the countess."

Anne made a face. "I'll see enough of them after Michael and I are married. Pray do not make me endure them until I must!"

"How did the countess take the news, by the way?"

"She swallowed it, though it went down a trifle sourly, I should think. The major result seems to be that now she's determined to marry Matty to a marquess at the very least. They come to London with that intention in the autumn."

"And the earl?"

Anne smiled. "He is a dear, and pretends to be very gruff, but I know he's pleased."

"Is he still set upon St. Paul's? A Christmas wedding would be lovely."

"If you're hoping to divert me entirely, hope again, my love," Anne warned. "I will have the reason for your glum looks, Di, and if you do not tell me, I'll be forced to quiz you without mercy."

"Oh, it's simply that everything is so flat and dull, with almost everyone gone to summer in the country."

"Nonsense." Anne hesitated a moment, for she had not yet broached the subject of Roger. Her return to London had found

Diana listless and pale, forcing an interest in the details of Mary's wedding and disinclined to other conversation. Thus far Anne had respected her avoidance of Roger's name, but now she felt she had to approach the topic. Diana really was beginning to look ill. "You may talk to me, you know," she said gently. "There is no danger of my telling anyone. You may trust me."

Diana reached out and squeezed her hand. "I know that, you ninny." She smiled fondly.

"It is Roger, is it not?"

Diana looked away.

"It needed saying, my love."

"It's no use!" Diana sprang to her feet and began to pace the strip of lawn. "I am eaten up with worry and guilt, and there is nothing to be done for it. He never even said good-bye—" She pulled out a folded slip of paper. "He wrote, in the coldest possible terms, to say he was leaving. There is no hope in this letter, none at all. I know he believes he'll be killed, and will do nothing toward his own safety, and—and—"

"Diana!" exclaimed Anne. "You *are* in love with him!"

The only answer was a muffled sob.

"Oh, my poor Di! I had not thought—I'd hoped so much, and Michael and I talked of it—but you both seemed so indifferent. Oh, Di!"

"Indifference! That is all I may hope for," Diana said and sniffed. "I cannot bear it. If only I knew him safe—oh, it's all my fault!" She looked at Anne with tear-filled eyes. "That night of your birthday ball—how well I have been repaid for my pride! How amply I suffer for my folly and wickedness! If only he comes home safely, I'll tell the truth to the whole world!"

This was a little much for Anne's good sense. "Don't be silly. There will be no need for that, I assure you. Come, sit here beside me and we'll puzzle out what to do."

"I will endure any humiliation, any mockery—I will gladly be slighted by everyone—ridiculed, disgraced, despised—"

"That is the outside of enough! What you need is a change of air and scenery. Yes, that is the very thing. You and I shall go to Mama at Midfield. They are all at sixes and sevens there after the weddings, with nothing to do, and Mama has been asking this age for me to bring you to her. You will like it above all things," she concluded firmly. "These ridiculous notions shall leave your mind at once, if you please. Now, dry your eyes and we'll go back into the house, and I'll write to Mama directly. She and Elizabeth and the twins will think of a dozen ways to amuse you."

A flicker of interest showed in the drowning green eyes. "Do you think—?"

"I most certainly do. Our country air will put the roses back in your cheeks. And it's as good a time as any to see the house, since you'll be its mistress some day soon," Anne finished with a sly smile.

Lord Bellrose was applied to and gave his permission for the two young ladies to set out the very next day. He had been concerned about his daughter's lack of spirits and alarmed when the gift of an emerald bracelet had elicited only a feeble smile and listless thanks. Her absence from London would, moreover, leave him free to have long conferences with Cousin Charles over the nuptial contracts.

Thus at a very early hour a carriage set out for Midfield, carrying Anne, Diana, their maids, a formidable amount of luggage, presents for the Rushden ladies, and those of Diana's jewels suitable for country wearing. Two grooms rode beside the equippage and another sat with the coachman on the box, and it had been with difficulty that Diana had restrained her father from calling upon some of his friends in the Guards to accompany them and see to their safety.

The journey proceeded smoothly, the ladies passing most of the time in playing piquet. The presence of the maids precluded any intimate conversation, but each was glad of this; Anne because she was not sure how much to say, and Diana because she wished to nurse her sore heart in peace.

As the neighbourhood of Midfield approached, Anne put the cards away in her reticule and pointed out the various landmarks and places of interest. Diana admired the countryside, the woods, the fine houses glimpsed beyond the trees, the vast folding downs, and gradually grew more excited at the prospect of coming to know these places intimately. Anne's teasing remark about her eventually becoming mistress of Midfield's broad acres and lush woods was uppermost in her mind, and while she did not entirely believe in the event, she could not help the extra interest the possibility caused in her.

They swept up the drive in late afternoon, to be welcomed by the entire family in residence, starting with Lady Rushden.

"My dear," her ladyship murmured, kissing Diana's cheek. "You are very welcome. Come inside and rest. I know you must be fatigued."

"Thank you, Lady Rushden," Diana said gratefully. She had been told by Anne that her ladyship would have welcomed with open arms any bride for her son, but that Diana was not Lady Matilda predisposed Roger's mother to adoration. Still, Diana felt that the welcome was truly sincere. They had all met a few years previously on Diana's short visit to Midfield, but the alteration in circumstances now made them treat her as one of the family, which she found very pleasant.

The country air did Diana good, as Anne had predicted. Long walks, rides about the estate, and the simple pleasures of life away from town restored much of her bloom. And here, in Roger's home, she felt much closer to him. Freed of uninterrupted social obligations and her father's lectures about money and property, she had the time to think and reflect. While constant occupation had only served to worsen her moods, solitude and quiet began to mend, if not her love, then at least her spirits.

For love Roger she did. She realised it now, surrounded by his family and taken into the embrace of his ancestral home. She cursed the weeks she had spent in avoiding his company, for the time might have been better spent in conversation and personal discovery. Yet the serenity of the wide fields, the winding river, and the sloping green lawns forbade excessive self-recriminations, for here she felt that Roger would indeed return to her. There would be time to win him.

Her confidence restored, her superstitious fears for Roger assuaged, Diana applied herself to learning the characters of his relations. Anne was her guide in this, although unbeknownst to that young lady, for from Anne's qualities she could trace those of Elizabeth, Caroline, and Catherine, and from all four sisters, their mother. She found much virtue and little silliness in the younger girls, although Caroline stood in awe of Diana's London clothes and manners, and Catherine never tired of hearing about parties, dinners, and balls. Diana indulged them both smilingly. Elizabeth was more subdued, but since Diana had heard the tale of her hopeless love for Lord Gerald, and since her own situation was so emotionally similar, she made a special effort to distract the girl from her melancholy.

Lady Rushden was another matter. Autocratic, though not as oppressively dictatorial as her elder sister the duchess, she seemed at first to be torn between a genuine liking for Diana and her reluctance to admit that sooner or later, Diana would replace her at Midfield. She foresaw thirty years of rule undone in a week, for the servants would know where their future lay and would begin to switch allegiances. She was soon and happily disabused of this notion, however, as Diana scrupulously avoided giving orders to any servant but her own maid. Within a few days Lady Rushden had so far relaxed as to give Diana a day-long tour of the house and its marvels, identifying each portrait, explaining each point of architecture, and even initiating her into the secrets of several passageways put in during the Civil Wars, the existence of which was still kept from all but the family. Her ladyship was by no means reconciled to handing over control of the house, but as her authority remained undamaged and even unchallenged, she gradually forgot her unease and began to love Diana for herself.

Local society besieged them. Although conversation revolved exclusively around horses, hunting, and land, Diana found that beneath the occasional nervous pretensions and limited chatter was the real backbone of the English spirit: honesty, good humour, and a love of their country that was to her mind a much more genuine form of patriotism than that to be found in London. When these people asserted that they would die for their nation, they referred not to any government or even to the Crown, but the rich fields and forests that rooted them and their families for countless generations into the very soil of England.

Diana was accorded every deference due the affianced bride of Lord Rushden. When she was found to be sensible in her speech, devoid of snobbery, possessed of a pretty laugh to go with her pretty face, and ready to join in their country pursuits despite her London upbringing, she was pronounced to be exactly the wife Roger needed.

This was not the opinion of the guests who came one day in the company of Lord and Lady Plowswyck. The countess of Chetley and her daughter, needing to discuss wedding plans with Lady Rushden, arrived intending to spend at least a week. The spectacle of her hostess making much of Roger's betrothed so soured the digestions of those who felt that Matilda should rightly be filling the role was a source of amusement to everyone—except Elizabeth, who could barely force herself to be civil. Diana, hiding her grins, spent much time giggling in private with Anne and wondering if Matilda would seek a battle with her. Of course, she did.

The encounter took place in the library, where Diana had gone to replace the first volume of a novel and to avail herself of the second. Lady Matilda chose her moment and followed her inside the room, closing the doors firmly. Diana turned, not particularly surprised, and smiled.

"You take much pleasure in reading, Lady Diana?" Lady Matilda asked, approaching to peer at the title of the book.

"A diversion most suited to me, though I feel guilty that I do not spend more time at it."

"It must be difficult, living at the very hub of London society." Lady Matilda glanced up at the tall rows of books. "The Rushdens are all great readers. Miss Elizabeth, especially. I scarcely see her without a book in her hands."

Diana forebore pointing out that burying one's nose in a book was an excellent barrier to conversation. "She is quite well informed on many subjects, I believe," was her sweet reply.

"You and I, of course, being acquainted with Society, know that such excess of information does not necessarily recommend one."

"Neither," Diana could not help responding, "does an excess of ignorance."

"Naturally. But you will agree, I know, that most gentlemen do not appreciate young ladies who are better informed than they. Lord Gerald has said to me many times that he is often dismayed by the accomplishments of some ladies."

Wisely, Diana bit back the obvious comment that he need not fear on Lady Matilda's account, and simply said, "Every man has a different taste."

"And what news from Lord Rushden?" Lady Matilda asked archly. "The family are great writers as well, I believe."

"Then I shall fit in very poorly, for I am a terrible correspondent. I suppose my lord will have occasion to upbraid me for my lack, once we are married." Diana smiled benevolently. "And you have reminded me that I've been neglecting my poor father. I really should write to him at once."

"I vow he was most surprised to hear of your engagement," Lady Matilda went on, not taking the hint. "So were we all, of course. I was apprised of it by his sister, Miss Anne Rushden. Can you guess under what circumstances, dear Lady Diana?"

"Truly, I cannot," Diana replied dulcetly.

"The circumstances were these: I had come to visit for a few days with my mother, the countess—"

"You must do so again whenever the earl can spare you from Chetley," Diana interrupted. "Roger and I will be so happy to have you here, as our sister-by-marriage, through Anne."

The contest was unequal, Diana observed with an inner giggle. Lady Matilda turned red, then sniffed delicately. "I thank you. You need not trouble on my account."

"Oh, it would be one of our chiefest pleasures, I assure you! We must love you for Anne's and Michael's sakes, in addition to your own character." Diana settled in to really enjoy herself. "Roger speaks so highly of your character."

"Did he also tell you that he proposed marriage to me, in this very house, when he had already engaged himself to you?"

Her smile did not waver even as a remembered voice mocked her—Roger's, saying that any young lady of quality would have done him as a fiancée. Diana sighed. "I beg you will forgive him. The nature of the commitment being secret, he had certain . . . shall we say, certain roles to play? Among them being that of 'unattached bachelor.'" She gave a little laugh. "Why, so many times I found myself in a similar situation, listening to proposals made me by delightful young men whom I knew well would report my refusal to all our friends." She shook her head. "So tedious, to be importuned thus! Yet so necessary in my position! I do regret any inconvenience this may have caused you, dear Lady Matilda, but Roger must have been certain of your refusal or he never would have asked." She watched this hit home and smiled. "I shall remonstrate with him directly upon his return, you may depend upon it. And he'll apologise for his shocking usage of you. Men are such provoking creatures, are they not?"

Lady Matilda was quite unequal to reply, which suited Diana completely. Linking her arm with the other lady's, she walked her to the door and opened it. "Yes, you must come visit us here at Midfield. Roger is such a wretch, but I trust to your perspicacity to understand his actions. And I'm sure you'll forgive him, and then we may have many happy times on your visits here."

"I shall look forward to it," Lady Matilda managed. Then, rallying, she added, "I'm sure Lord Gerald will be most happy to accept as well. You know of course that he and I . . ."

"Yes?" Diana encouraged, not so amused now.

"Yes," Lady Matilda purred. "Naturally. It is quite certain now. My parents need only be informed, and after that—"

"My congratulations," Diana said coldly. Then, as inspiration hit, she went on, "I shall have to convey my felicitations to Lord Gerald as well, the next time I see him."

"Have you met him, then?"

"Oh, of course. He is a most frequent visitor to Midfield," Diana improvised, since she had never set eyes on the man in her life. "And a great favourite with all the ladies here." After another sweet smile, she propelled Lady Matilda out of the room with a gentle push. "Now, I really must write to my father. You leave tomorrow, I think? Then I shall see you at dinner."

Diana watched Lady Matilda stumble slightly over a minuscule unevenness in the carpet of the hall, and swiftly turned away to conceal a grin. Closing the doors of the library, she collapsed into a chair and laughed into a pillow for some time.

But when she finally opened the book, she could not settle to it. A romantic novel is a poor substitute for the object of one's personal romantic feelings, and she fell to counting the days since Roger had left for Portugal. Restlessly she tossed the book aside and decided to take a walk down to the riverbank. Elsewhere in the house, she knew, plans were proceeding for Anne's wedding gown and the debate between pearls, diamonds, and sapphires as her jewels. Thoughts of another's nuptials naturally disposed Diana to consideration of her own. She walked slowly down the riverbank, pretending that it was the aisle of Midfield's charming little Norman church, picked enough wildflowers for a respectable bouquet, and dreamed of white tulle starred with brilliants. Roger would wear his uniform, of course, his hair as golden as the trimming of his coat. It took no effort to conjure a picture of him and she took it with her to the riverbank, sitting down on a flat rock to laze and dream in the summer warmth. She could almost see him nearby, bending over the river to splash cool water on his face, shaking his head like a wet puppy, droplets flying around him as he laughed, reaching out a hand to her—

The very real sound of hoofbeats took her abruptly from her daydream. There, on the opposite bank, a tall young man was dismounting from a big grey gelding. But his hair was brown and his build not so lean as Roger's. Diana sighed quietly and stayed quite still on her rock. Her patterned green gown blended into the colours of the foliage, and the rock was sheltered by a little thicket of berry brambles, so she was confident that he had not seen her. But as he bent over the water to splash himself, exactly as she had pictured Roger, she bit her lip and turned away. When she finally looked back, at hearing his happy laugh, her eyes rounded. For he was holding out his hand to Elizabeth.

Diana gasped and shrank back into the shrubbery. She absently noted a second horse, now cropping grass near the gelding, and the riding habit Elizabeth wore, and suddenly all those lone horseback expeditions that Diana had been politely discouraged from joining became clear. She hadn't lied to Lady Matilda after all, she thought dazedly. Lord Gerald, it seemed, was a *very* frequent visitor to Midfield.

Diana felt the pull very strongly of two opposing emotions. She longed to be embraced by Roger as Lord Gerald was now embracing Elizabeth, but she also knew that what they were doing was wrong and could lead to a horrifying scandal. She waited and watched, and presently the pair drew apart and Elizabeth began to coil up her tumbled blond hair.

Lord Gerald reached into his pocket and produced a piece of paper. He unfolded it and showed it to Elizabeth. She read it, faltered, and gazed up at him in the leaf-shaded coolness of the river with her arms lifting to go around his neck.

Diana had seen enough. "Elizabeth!"

The blond hair cascaded again as Elizabeth's head snapped around in astonishment. Diana scrambled to her feet, but the heel of her slipper caught in the hem of her gown and she cried out as her ankle twisted painfully. Righting herself with difficulty, she called out Elizabeth's name again.

The pair on the opposite bank hurried to their horses. They were mounted before Diana could cry out again, and Elizabeth shouted, "Give my love to Roger!" before she and Lord Gerald rode up the bank and into the trees.

Diana almost screamed with frustration. Every step was exquisite agony as she made her way as quickly as she could back to the house. She caught her skirts up in her hands and tried to run, but her ankle twisted from under her and she fell. Finally, her left foot able to support her for only scant seconds as she hobbled up the lawns, she gained the back terrace. Through the drawing room she limped, intending to go straight to Lady Rushden.

Instead, in the hall, she found her hostess, Anne, and the countess and Lady Matilda on their way downstairs.

"Di!" Anne hurried to her side. "Whatever is the matter? Your ankle? Poor thing!"

"Are you all right, Diana my dear?" Lady Rushden helped Anne ease her into a chair at the foot of the steps. "Oh, good gracious, it's swelling. Anne, find Calvert and have him send round to the doctor. And we need cold cloths at once."

Diana looked from one to the other, and then to the Chetley ladies. She could not so expose this family to disgrace. And as she thought it over while a cold compress was applied to her swollen ankle, she began to take a perverse delight in the secret she had so unwittingly discovered. A few hours alone together on a ride was not so very great a thing, after all. To tattle on the pair would only send riders out after them, Elizabeth would be in terrible trouble with her Mama, and Lord Gerald would be forbidden the house— and Lady Matilda would probably make a frightful scene, which would end in an insistence upon marriage that instant. Perhaps, she thought with a grimace as her foot was elevated onto another chair, perhaps Lady Matilda would be so insulted that she would re- nounce Lord Gerald. But Diana felt certain that she would never countenance the loss of not one, but two eligible young men, and would somehow force poor Lord Gerald into marriage with her. No, it was best not to say anything at all, she decided, and hope that Elizabeth and her lover would defy everyone by becoming publicly engaged very soon.

Diana was assisted up to her room, ensconced on a pile of pillows in bed, and left alone until the doctor came, which suited her very well. When he pronounced her ankle to be simply wrenched, not broken, and prescribed cold compresses, no activ- ity, and sleep, she took the draught he gave her and settled happily to fulfill his advice, never dreaming of the trouble her silence would cause.

# === 15 ===

MICHAEL LEANED BACK against a tree and sighed. He and Roger had indulged in lunch and a full wineskin and were now cheerfully arguing tactics with the artillery officer accompanying them on their tour of the Portuguese countryside. A civilian, Mr. Avery, was the fourth member of their little group, chosen for the expedition because of a single qualification: fluent Portuguese. Michael grinned at the translator, who was hunched over a Swedish grammar. The country scholar had decided that war service to his country would not interrupt the addition of a seventh language to his collection. He did not share the enthusiasm of the other young men for this secret mission, and a combination of hot climate and prior sedentary years served to tire him more quickly than his companions.

Another group of four from the ship was traversing the hills some miles distant. Not one of them had ever set foot in Portugal before, and all that most of them knew about the country was that it produced port wine and cork. Mr. Avery and the other translator, Mr. Willits, had attempted to give shipboard lectures, but their only audience had been Michael. The entire rest of the party had been miserably seasick, and at times during his unwonted foray back into the schoolroom, Michael had wished the same fate on himself. The only item of interest to him was that the Portuguese nobility had only ceased eating with its fingers in 1744, when forks had been introduced from London.

Their task for the War Ministry was simple enough: locate the bands of mountain *guerrilleros* currently making Marshal Junot's life a misery, and enlist same in the battle Wellesley was planning for August. What the Minister had not mentioned was that the search would be conducted on foot.

Michael had breathed more dust, suffered more heat, walked more miles in badly woven sandals, and slept on harder ground than he had believed humanly possible. But he had also observed unspoiled natural beauty, bathed in cool streams, enjoyed remarkably pungent local cheese and wine, and gazed at enchanting vistas of mountain, forest, and valley. The only real drawback for him was the language. Roger had picked up a smattering of Portuguese, but Michael was hopeless with any tongue other than the King's English. Portuguese vowels in particular eluded him completely. He was incapable of the slurring, gargling, swallowing, nasalizing, and mangling necessary to reproduction of even the simplest terms. So while Roger and Mr. Mitchells, the artilleryman, attended to Mr. Avery's conversations with the villagers, Michael put his time to what was for him a much more beneficial use: he dreamed about Anne.

He had withdrawn from the discussion of Napoleon's victory at Friedland for just that purpose. There was a certain type of grass growing on the sunbaked hills that had turned golden over the last month, reminding him forcibly of his beloved's silken hair. He shaded his eyes with his lashes, comparing the cloudless blue sky to her eyes, the little wild roses along the pathways to her cheeks, and other romantic effusions that would have pleased her endlessly and that would have brought howls of laughter from any man not similarly in love. Which was why he never talked to Roger about Diana.

". . . so you see," Roger was saying to Mr. Mitchells when Michael finally came out of his waking dream, "it will not do to sit ponderously by while Bonaparte strikes at us with lightning speed. If we do, we'll lose."

"That's as may be, m'lord," Mitchells allowed. "But for my money, British bullheadedness will win out in the long view."

Michael grinned. Which, he wondered, possessed it in greater measure: Roger, or Diana?

"I trust you're right, Mr. Mitchells. Sooner or later we'll bring that madman to his knees. But a change in tactics would bring it about much faster."

Mitchells excused himself and walked down to the trickling stream to wash. Michael, lounging back against his tree, frowned at seeing his friend's expression change to one of bleakness. "Roger? What is it?"

"I only wish I could be here to see it happen."

"Oh, God!" Michael groaned. "Back on that, are you? When Annie told me to take care of you, she didn't say I'd be dealing with a lunatic! But never mind, we'll all have the laugh of you when we toast your ninetieth birthday."

"God forbid!" Roger suddenly laughed. "You'd wish decrepitude on me? I appreciate the thought, but I should like to leave a rather more attractive corpse."

"Vanity, vanity," Michael said with a sigh. "Anyway, I am at leisure to be further diverted. The prospect of your wizened corpse bores me, Roger. Think up something amusing." He paused deliberately. "Our fair Diana, for instance. You never did say how she bid you farewell."

"There were no farewells at all."

"What?" He opened his eyes wide in exaggerated surprise. "No tender parting barbs? No solicitous insults? No gentle remonstrations to keep your golden hide intact, so that she might have the pleasure of skinning you alive herself?"

Roger shot him a murderous look. "Have done, Michael."

"Nothing of the kind," Michael went on. A furious Roger was better than a despondent one. Rivers of champagne, card tables, and gypsy singers being unavailable, the subject of Diana was nicely calculated to rouse a suitable rage. Michael pursued his goal mercilessly. "I am scandalised. I am speechless with amazement."

"A baldfaced lie, more's the pity."

"How could you have missed such an opportunity?" Michael folded his arms behind his head in an attitude of daydreaming, keeping one careful eye on Roger. "Think on it. What proofs of her regard must be taken from her insolence! Consider the surety of her tenderest feelings, which must be yours with every venomous glance! Ah, would that Anne were so eloquent in her incivility in order to prove her love!"

Goaded, Roger scowled and began a hot retort. But then a cunning look passed over his face, followed by an expression of sheer mischief. "Indeed," he said slowly. "My lady's eagerness to convince me of her adoration surpasses Anne's any day. Diana quit town altogether rather than tell me good-bye, and who could take such a demonstration as anything but proof of the most deep and passionate regard?"

Michael roared with laughter, puzzling Mr. Mitchells, returning just then from the stream. Describing the cause of the hilarity was impossible, so Michael got to his feet, hauled Roger upright, and organised the little group to set forth once more.

They had met with nothing but the most ardent welcome wherever they appeared. If there was anything the Portuguese hated more than they hated the Spanish, it was the French. Marshal Junot's patrols from Lisbon had not been appreciated. Roger had added to their arsenal of blandishments the idea that by driving the French out of Portugal, Spain would thus be gifted with the loathed soldiers of Napoleon. This proved the clinching factor, and in the last month they had added up the total of armed and vindictive *guerrilleros* to a highly satisfying number. Wellesley might bring in his crack British troops, but in the battle and along the French flanks would be these Portuguese—ill mounted on their sturdy ponies, ill armed, untrained, only marginally organised—and rabid in their hatred of the French.

After they had been on their way for about an hour, Roger stopped to pick the stones out of his sandals. "I should have gone to sea," he complained. "No trails to follow, no hard ground to sleep on, no rocks! The cool foam in one's face, fresh air, a comfortable cot—and only think how well the uniform would have suited me."

"Nonsense," Michael answered. "You lost your dinner five minutes after we boarded ship, and we hadn't even left Portsmouth."

"Nelson got seasick," Roger said defensively.

"Only because he had but one arm to steady himself. Do come along, Roger, or we'll not reach the next hovels by nightfall."

"God, more olives, and more garlic!"

"Shh!" Mr. Mitchells was a few yards ahead of them on the narrow trail through the woods, his attitude that of a hound quivering after a scent. He gestured for them to leave the rutted path, and they obediently melted into the undergrowth.

Safely hidden, their dull clothes adequate camouflage, Michael whispered, "What is it?"

"Horses."

The natives used surefooted, strong ponies for travel and farming. The tall, slim-boned Thoroughbred was unsuited to this terrain; yet it was upon such nervous, arrogant animals that a file of riders appeared around a narrow curve. Their dusty uniforms were French.

Michael asked Roger a question with his eyes. Four British against ten Frenchmen and their high-strung horses—was it worth it? he asked silently. It would be impossible for the French to mass against them on the trail, since bushes and trees began only a few yards to either side of it. The horses would have been trained to gunfire, of course, but also to open field battle, not this nerve-racking enclosure. The French would not be expecting resistance, let alone concealed marksmen in the bushes. Roger gave a tight, feral grin, which Michael returned, and they set about loading their pistols.

The French patrol chose a shady spot about a hundred yards off to rest and drink. None dismounted. Complaints were muttered among them, and they were supremely oblivious to the English, who held a hurried conference in whispers and then steathily arranged themselves along the undergrowth with two pistols each.

"That's enough," the French leader said in a bored voice. "Maybe we can take care of these louts and be finally back in Lisbon before night. *Merde,* this dust! What a disgusting country! I hope that girl was right, André."

André turned his head. "It was only rumour," he ventured. "Should we not take the information back to Marshal Junot?"

"So you can rest your lousy behind on a soft chair? You've waited a week; you can wait while we find and capture the imbecile English. And just think how pleased Monsieur le Marechal will be to have an English spy in his hands! We'll learn every plan they have.

Well, come on, let's go."

Michael peered through his chosen bush at Roger, seeing the same thoughts flickering in the blue eyes. They could not allow these men to get away and make any report to Junot. Their disappearance would be remarked upon, of course, but probably attributed to the Portuguese *guerrilleros*. Michael hefted his custom-made Mantons—duelling pistols, useless in battle but perfect for shots like this—and waited.

The leader wiped his brow and heeled his grey mare around to lead his troop off again, single file down the slender path. Michael counted carefully. His were the seventh and eighth riders, and as the fifth horse passed him he pointed his pistols through the concealing leaves. Sweat ran into his eyes and he blinked it away. As the sixth rider passed him a smile began on his face and he took unerring aim.

Three shots rang out, so close together as to be heard as one, and then a fourth, belated firing from Mr. Avery. Four French uniforms toppled from their saddles and thrashed in the dusty road. Before any of the remaining French could do more than curse in surprise, four more shots were fired, each one distinct this time. Michael, having killed both his men, tossed the guns down and crashed through the bushes to the road. It was time for a more direct form of battle, and the first thing he required was a sword.

Mr. Avery had missed his second shot entirely, and Mr. Mitchells had only winged the fourth rider, so the four British faced four Frenchmen, one slightly wounded. The danger was from the pistols strapped to the hips of the four survivors; Michael used a struggling horse as cover to keep himself from perforation as a shot was directed at him. He rolled to the ground, hurriedly unsheathing the sword from the belt of the dead man on the ground, as the horse lurched to its feet and galloped off. Scrambling to get his own legs under him, Michael turned to find himself faced with the French leader, and smiled.

This was not one of Bonaparte's peasant recruits taught in a week how to fire a gun. The sabre sliced out of its scabbard, and the elegant stance of the born swordsman was adopted. Michael saluted the man mockingly. He learned in the first moments of the encounter what he had suspected from the man's stance; the Frenchman knew what he was about. They fought on, not heeding the shouts and clashes of steel around them, the plunging horses, the shrieks that meant wounds had been scored. Michael much preferred close combat to guns; it was exhilarating to match one's wits and skills against another's. But as he worked, enjoying himself and respecting his opponent, he began to gain the advantage without having to exert himself very hard for it. The Frenchman was capable, but out of condition. Michael pressed him back into the shallow ditch along the side of the trail, testing, feinting, grinning. Weeks of easy, wine-soaked living in Lisbon showed in the rounded belly, the flushed face, the sweating expenditure of energy that slowed the Frenchman's reactions and made him awkward. Although they seemed about the same age, Michael had had a month of toughening exertion behind him and was in better shape to begin with. Pursuing his opponent contemptuously into the brush, when the man made a foolish, desperate move, Michael ran him through.

He pulled the sword from the uniformed chest—a good, clean heart-thrust that had killed instantly—and without pausing to wipe the blade whirled to see where Roger was. Mr. Avery was nearby, valiantly but ineptly defending himself from a not particularly skilled swordsman. Michael yelled an insult in bad French, the only one he knew and the only one he had ever needed in battle, to make the man turn. He had no taste for sheathing his blade in an enemy's back, even a Frenchman's. But as the trooper's free hand fumbled at his belt during his slow turn, Michael stiffened. Before he could throw himself out of the way, there was a pistol pointed straight at his heart.

A smile danced in the little black eyes, and the finger tightened around the trigger. Michael held his breath, transfixed. The Frenchman pitched forward like a felled tree, his dead finger moving in spasm, the pistol discharging harmlessly into the ground.

"Have a care, Michael!" Roger called as he wrenched his sword from between the dead man's ribs. "Anne would never forgive me!"

"Roger!"

"Look after the rest of them for me, there's a good fellow," Roger yelled as he ran after the only horse left in the clearing, its reins wrapped around the wrist of a dead Frenchman. As he undid the leather and vaulted lightly into the saddle, Michael saw the spreading bloodstain on Roger's left thigh. "One got away, and I'm going after him!"

"Wait! Roger, damn you, wait!"

But Roger was off, back the way the French had come. Michael cursed again, telling himself it was just Roger's bloody luck to grab the only horse. He ignored Mr. Avery, who was stammering out thanks for the rescue and an apology for placing Michael in so much danger, and surveyed the debris. All the French were either dead or close enough to it to make no difference, except for the one Roger had gone after. Michael ground his teeth.

"Mitchells! Where's Mitchells?"

"Here, m'lord!"

He followed the weak voice to an impressive pile of bodies. Mitchells was alive at the bottom, and Michael yanked the four dead Frenchmen aside and knelt to inspect the young man's wounds. "Let's have a look, shall we? Avery! Bring some water, won't you? Ah, here we are—right through the shoulder, and from the look of it, not even a nick to your collarbone. Avery!" He shouted again, peering at the slice taken out of Mitchells's side. "That's not bad, either. You've flesh enough there. Swords leave a nasty scar, but it'll be something interesting to show your ladies, eh?" He grinned bracingly at the young man, who smiled feebly back.

"Oh, that's all right, then," Mitchells murmured, and fainted.

"Avery!" Michael bellowed again. "Where's the damned water?"

But Mr. Avery, released at last from the outrageous demands on his placid scholarly soul, had followed Mitchells's example, with mush less cause, and was sprawled unconscious in the road.

Michael swore feelingly, looked up the trail to where Roger had disappeared, and swore again. Then he climbed wearily to his feet and set about reviving Mr. Avery, making Mitchells comfortable, and burying the dead.

# =16=

DIANA'S ANKLE, SUFFICIENTLY swollen and painful to preclude her coming down at all the next day, provided her with an unexpected refuge. She had begun the morning with tea and toast brought up by her maid and imagining the most romantic scenes between Elizabeth and Lord Gerald. These crumbled into dust when Anne arrived shortly after nine o'clock, and in the greatest distress.

"We can't find Elizabeth," she said worriedly. "I know she's been avoiding Lady Matilda and the countess, but this is absurd. She isn't in her room, and her bed hasn't been slept in. Caro and Cathy seem to think she's ridden off to stay with some neighbour or other for a few days, until Lady Matilda is gone, but it isn't like Lizzie simply to disappear without a word."

Diana buttered her toast and said nothing.

"She's been in such dumps lately," Anne went on, shaking her head. "We've been trying to bring Mama round, and I've told her that Lizzie may have my portion—since Michael is so very rich we won't need what Roger would have given me—but Mama only frowns and makes noises about going penniless to one's bridegroom—as if I cared for that!"

"Michael would have you barefoot, in homespun," Diana observed with a slight smile.

"Well, I suppose so," Anne said, and blushed. "Still, I'd gladly give Lizzie whatever Roger would have settled on me if he'd stayed around long enough to write the contracts himself. As it is, the earl's man of business and Roger's have been at it this age. I'm seriously considering an elopement when Michael returns."

The word "elopement" made Diana choke on her toast. Suddenly she knew what had happened to Elizabeth and Lord Gerald. And, horrified, she also knew that she herself would be sunk the moment they returned. She could just hear them thanking her for not raising the alarm and causing them to be apprehended.

"Diana? Are you all right? Is your ankle paining you again? Here, why don't I pour you some more of the medicine the doctor left you."

"Oh, please," Diana said faintly, and spent the rest of the morning in uneasy slumber.

By the time Anne appeared with Diana's tea tray, the whole house was in an uproar. Elizabeth had not been found at any of the neighbours'; no one on any of the roads had seen her. Anne revealed all this to Diana, but not the morbid speculation that ran rampant at Midfield. This Diana had to find out for herself when she limped downstairs the next morning, supported by a slim hardwood cane.

She was greeted kindly in the morning room, her health and spirits enquired after, and was settled onto a sopha with her foot propped on an embroidered stool. All these attentions served to make her excruciatingly uncomfortable in her mind, especially when conversation lapsed back into worries about what could have become of Elizabeth.

"Perhaps Lady Penny is hiding her for the duration," Caro suggested hopefully. "They're great friends, you know."

She was quickly hushed by her mother and sisters, who made significant glances in Lady Matilda's direction where she sat near the windows, ostensibly reading. But Diana caught the faintest twitch of expression on her face, and scowled.

"Perhaps she's been stolen by gypsies!" Catherine exclaimed.

Lady Rushden tossed her hands, and the handkerchief she had been halfheartedly embroidering, into the air. "My God! How could two intelligent persons like Rushden and myself produce such children? How miraculously unburdened you are, both of you, by the inconvenience of brains!"

Lady Matilda coughed. Diana glared at her from behind a handful of tatting, but stayed silent. The countess then ventured her own opinion, which was that Elizabeth might have been waylaid by villains and was even now lying in some ditch, unconscious. This helpful, happy thought met with the cold silence it deserved, the excuse for this chilling reception being the entrance of Calvert with the morning post. The silver salver was placed on a table, ignored after Calvert informed her ladyship that there was nothing on it that bore Miss Elizabeth's handwriting, and forgotten.

"If I may be allowed to say so, my lady," Calvert directed at his mistress, "we are all most distressed belowstairs and share your apprehensions as to Miss Elizabeth's eventual fate."

Diana stared at him. Anne gulped and pressed a handkerchief to her face. Lady Rushden thanked him frigidly for his concern and told him to leave. And Lady Matilda, at the windows with her book, unmistakably coughed.

Diana clenched her teeth and counted to one hundred and twenty before she could reasonably trust herself to speak. "I feel sure, Lady Rushden, that Elizabeth is all right. Surely if the news were bad, we should have heard something by now."

"Thank you for trying to raise my spirits, my dear Diana, but with every hour I confess my hopes sink further. Where can she have gone? What can have befallen her? She's not a foolish girl by any means. She would never have gone off alone, without a word to anyone."

Diana swallowed painfully, about to confess what she had seen. She was saved from this fatal idiocy by Lady Matilda, who rose from her window seat and said, "I fear we are *de trop,* Mother." Diana winced at her French accent. "Perhaps we should order our packing so that we may not burden this unhappy family with any obligations to our entertainment."

"How kind of you to say so," Anne said through a valiantly forced smile. "But you need not go on our account."

"Indeed, no," Lady Rushden seconded dimly.

"I realise that my presence may have been . . . painful . . . to Miss Elizabeth," Lady Matilda went on inexorably. "If I have been the cause of her running away, I should never forgive myself. Simply that a gentleman prefers one lady to another is no reason to be so dramatic as to flee. But I made every effort to befriend Miss

Elizabeth, and I fear very much that she might have taken my efforts amiss and become offended. It could only be good in me to remove myself from Midfield at once, so that when she returns, she may not be presented with the sight of someone who—''

"Oh, really, Matilda!" Anne burst out. Diana, who had been speculating on the chances of marrying off Matilda to Young George, since they certainly deserved each other and would understand and complement each other perfectly, actually jumped in her seat. "I never heard such nonsense in all my life! If you ask me, Lizzie is much more likely to have run off either to or with Lord Gerald than to be lying in a ditch somewhere!" She finished with a glare at her future mother-in-law.

"Anne!" Lady Rushden exclaimed.

Diana, who had turned scarlet as Anne had hit on what she believed to be the precise truth, rallied and came to her friend's defence, both for the present harmony of those in the morning room and the future relationship of Anne with her intended relations. "I think we're all overwrought," she said firmly, shooting a warning glance at Anne. "We're all saying things we don't mean because of this terrible worry over Lizzie. I'm sure Lady Matilda didn't mean to imply anything, and I'm sure Anne will forgive her for what she actually didn't say, and I feel certain that Lady Matilda will be generous to her for saying what she did, for after all, they are to be sisters, are they not?''

This speech was sufficiently complex as to render everyone silent while they worked it all out. Diana covered the quiet by rising to her feet and going to the bell rope. When Calvert arrived, almost on the instant, she directed him to bring in coffee and something to eat. By the time all this was accomplished, those who had finally comprehended the meaning of Diana's words had decided to leave well enough alone, and those who did not understand a word she had said decided to behave as if they had. Everyone happily ignored the entire contretemps and talked of the weather for a full fifteen minutes.

Diana, at her ease once again on the sopha, congratulated herself and sighed in relief. Nothing would have given her more pleasure than to reveal to the assembled ladies that Anne's guess had been exactly right. Unfortunately, she had no way of knowing if *she* was right in her speculations. She knew what she had seen, and from the expressions on both Lord Gerald's and Elizabeth's faces, Gretna Green would most probably have been their destination, as it was for so many other couples for whom marriage in England was not swift enough. Diana mused that in all probability, Scotland had seen more British marriages than it had Scottish ones.

The untimely smile that this thought provoked was taken from her face by Calvert's reentrance into the morning room. He was ghastly white and stammering. But even as he struggled for words, the entrance of Elizabeth and Lord Gerald caused Lady Rushden to employ the full extent of her rather powerful voice.

"What is the meaning of this?" She sat bolt upright in her chair, her eyes popping out of her head.

Lord Gerald turned very red and answered bravely, "Allow me to make my apologies, my lady, and to introduce you to my wife, Lady Gerald."

"Wife?"

"What?"

"Impossible!"

This last from Lady Matilda. Diana, about to sink back onto the pillows with a heartfelt prayer of thanks for deliverance, suddenly yelped an order at Calvert. "Catch her! She's going to faint!"

The countess attended to her prostrate daughter while the Rushdens interspersed embraces and kisses with well-deserved abuse for the trouble Elizabeth had caused them. Diana, torn between watching the efforts of one family and the effusions of the other, could not make up her mind whether to laugh or merely smile. She finally gave up and giggled quietly to herself, thinking how much fun she and Anne were going to have relating the whole tale to Michael and Roger.

Lord Gerald presented the special licence and a copy of the marriage lines to his new mother-in-law, the latter of which showed that the wedding had taken place a mere two hours after Elizabeth had ridden away with him. With this proof of honourable intentions honourably carried out, Lady Rushden condescended to welcome his lordship into her family.

Explanations took no small amount of time. They were carried on in low voices at one end of the morning room, while at the other end application of burnt feathers and smelling salts had revived Lady Matilda into her mother's sympathetic embraces. Diana, straining her ears over the sobs of both Chetley ladies, learned that Elizabeth had overheard the end of Diana's conversation with Lady Matilda a few days before in the hall, and when Lord Gerald had arrived for their regular tryst and the special licence had been produced, she had indeed followed his directions to name the day. Which was that very day, of course, so as to secure him from the predatory and determined Lady Matilda.

"We were in terrors that someone would ride after us," Elizabeth confessed to Anne, casting a look at Diana, who blanched. "But no one did."

"But where have you been the last two days?" Anne scolded. "We've been horribly worried. It was very bad in you, Lizzie."

"I'm sorry for that, but—" She took her husband's hand and gazed at him adoringly. "It was likely to be the only wedding trip we'll ever have. We stayed at a little country inn. It was lovely."

Lady Rushden snorted. "Wedding trip indeed!" She rose and gazed sourly at her daughter. "Well, Lady Gerald, we still dine at the same time here. Caroline, Catherine, attend me to my rooms."

"Oh, Mama," they chorused plaintively. "May we not stay and talk with Lizzie? Please?"

Their mother looked an inch away from boxing both their ears. Instead she fixed a stony glare upon them. "All of you will come to ruin, every single one of you! If any of the rest of you behave in such a disgraceful manner, I shall have Roger transport you to the nearest convent." She turned to sweep from the room, then swung back around. "And will one of you please do something for Lady Matilda?"

It was to be expected that the desire of the Chetley ladies to remain upon the scene of the familial happiness was not great. In fact, the countess ordered their packing as soon as Lady Matilda had let go of her shoulders and appeared no longer to require her maternal bosom to cry onto. Diana helpfully assisted in their departure, giving Calvert the necessary instructions. No one thought to delay the countess or Lady Matilda, and they were gone within the hour.

The newly married pair had long since been escorted upstairs by the twins, their presence being naturally the primary source of Lady Matilda's tears. Once this removal was accomplished, after many fierce looks and whispers from Anne and Diana, things marched smoothly along. So smoothly, in fact, that when Anne finally collapsed onto a chair near Diana's sopha, the two young ladies could do nothing but stare at each other for several minutes. Then, because weeping seemed entirely out of order after the happy relief of Elizabeth's safe return and the scene played by Lady Matilda, both of them began to laugh.

"Oh, dear," Diana finally said with a gasp. "I'm so glad that didn't happen while the countess was still here!"

"It wouldn't matter in the least," Anne managed, waving her hands in front of her cheeks to cool them. "The Rushden name is now anathema at the castle! I shan't be allowed inside! Oh, but Di, did you see the look on her face?"

"Didn't you?" When Anne shook her head, Diana fell into fresh whoops. When she could speak again, she said, "My dear, she turned positively puce in the face—and looked exactly like a gigged frog!"

Anne tried to calm herself, failed, and got up to get them both a glass of sherry. "It really is too awful of us to laugh so," she confessed, still grinning. "But I can't say that I'm terribly unhappy with the outcome of it all."

Diana, accepting the sherry, nodded. "And wait until you hear what I've decided for Lady Matilda," she said with a giggle. "When next we're all in London together, I'm going to give the grandest ball you ever saw and introduce her—"

"My God! Not to Young George!" Anne nearly dropped her glass. "Oh, Di, you would not! Promise me I'll be there to see it!"

"Honour bright."

When their mirth had worn off and the sherry was gone, Anne went to replace the glasses and her eye fell on the salver holding the morning's post. She sorted through it, handed Diana a letter from her father, then picked up a clean butter knife from the tray of coffee and biscuits to slit an envelope addressed to her. Diana was scanning her father's illegible scrawl, which had mostly to do with the settlement Charles had arranged and which now wanted only Lord Rushden's signature, when Anne gave a choking cry.

"Oh, no!"

"Anne? What is it?"

"Oh God, no it can't be true, it can't be—"

"Anne!" Diana got up and limped to her friend's side. Anne was rocking gently back and forth, tears streaming down her cheeks. "Anne—" A terrible notion hit her. "It isn't Michael?"

Tormented blue eyes looked up at her. "Oh, Diana," Anne whispered.

Cold to her marrow, Diana held out her hand for the letter. Bracing herself with the cane, she squared her shoulders and took a deep breath. Michael's writing was uneven, splotched where a faulty pen had leaked and blotted the page.

> *My darling* (Michael had written),
> *On 21 August we fought the French at Vimiero and won a great victory. I am quite safe and uninjured but for a graze on my arm which did not even bleed much. But my dearest love, please prepare yourself and our Diana for what I must tell you now. We cannot find Roger. There was a small skirmish in the woods, where we killed nine Frenchmen on patrol. Roger went after the tenth man on horseback. He was wounded in the leg, but not seriously enough to keep him from riding, so I cannot think it was so great a wound. But no one has seen him or heard from him since. I had charge of the wounded men, one of them a hopeless imbecile named Avery who insisted we return to the coast and wait for the British landings. I will never forgive myself for not going after Roger, and I told myself at the time that he would ride after us and catch up, as he had a horse and we did not.*
> *Wherever we went I gave out his description and*

*begged the Portuguese to search for him. After Vimiero
I scoured the hills myself. He is not listed as prisoner or
wounded or dead. I simply cannot find him. It is as if
he vanished from the face of the earth.*

*The pain I feel as his friend can be nothing to what
you feel as his sister. Of Diana's feelings I dare not
think. I wish so much to be with you now, my Anne, but
will stay here as long as I am able and will try to find
Roger. Pray God I will succeed, and have hope. And
remember that I am always your loving*

*Michael*

Diana looked at the envelope, which had been addressed to the
duchess's house in London. It had been redirected to Midfield by
special express. Diana calculated back, reasoning that Michael had
probably written a few days after the battle. A week or more to get
the letter to England, she mused, another few days to the duchess,
another day here. Roger had therefore been missing for over a
fortnight. There should be another letter from Michael soon, Diana
told herself, and folded the pages. Slipping them back into the
envelope, she smoothed the creases made during its long journey
from Portugal. It was hot there, someone had told her, very hot and
humid, with a bright sun and gold-brown hills in September.
Roger's hair was gold, and his skin would be sunburned brown
from the long weeks in that bright, hot sun.

"Diana! Di!"

She looked at Anne, who stood beside her. "Yes?"

"Come upstairs, Di, and rest. Please, love, do."

"Oh, no." She smiled, curiously calm. "First I must write to my
father. We have connexions in various places, you know. And
Wellesley is an old friend of Papa's." She patted Anne's shoulder.
"Michael probably found Roger days ago. Don't look so downcast.
It's all to tease me, Anne. You know Roger."

Anne stared, worried and bewildered. "Di—"

"Don't worry," Diana said and smiled. "Michael will find him."
And she limped away to the library to write.

# —17—

MICHAEL DID NOT find him.

Instead he returned to England, under vigorous protest, with Arthur Wellesley. The victor of Vimiero had been summoned to London to face a court of enquiry regarding the terms given to the French after the battle.

> *Sir Hew Dalrymple* (Michael wrote before his departure from Portugal) *was irked at his own lateness, arriving as he did with fifteen thousand men well after the battle. He took command from Wellesley, who naturally must now go to England to explain why the French have been allowed out of Portugal scot-free. Still, we have managed to liberate the country with a single battle, and the peaceful withdrawal of the French will save many lives. And the Portuguese are ecstatic that their Spanish neighbours will have the frogs marching through their land and hope for much damage to Spain. But to ensure that the French really are leaving, British troops are being sent out hourly for inspection of every inch of Portugal. This will, I hope devoutly, help us find Roger. But I have been ordered home.*

Anne chewed her lower lip as she read this missive for the dozenth time. Diana's reaction to the news had been a small shrug and the comment that doubtless they would find Roger lolling in a villa overlooking the sea, taking the sun.

Sighing, Anne gazed out the window at the dusk. The uncertain light shadowed the trees, which bore the first signs of the coming winter. A servant came into the library to light the candles and stoke up the fire, and Anne could smell dinner from the kitchens. Life at Midfield went on as always, for all that its master might be dead.

Leaving the library, she wandered into the hall. She would have to dress for dinner soon, and had little desire to spend yet another meal listening to Diana's unconcerned chatter. Lady Rushden attributed Diana's lack of worry to shock and a defence against pain, but Anne was beginning to doubt that explanation. Surely there should have been some sign by now of anxiety on Roger's behalf. But Diana behaved as she had always done, and her example had infected everyone else over the weeks. Everyone, that is, except Anne.

The front door suddenly flew open, admitting a chill wind, a scatter of leaves—and Michael. Anne whirled round to snap angrily at whoever had let in such a draught, then cried out in joy and cast herself into her betrothed's arms.

He clasped her to him, muddy and filthy from the road as he was, and rained kisses on her face and hair. "Don't cry," he whispered, and she shook her head, not knowing that tears coursed down her cheeks. "Anne—darling, I'm home, don't cry." He drew away from her slightly. "Where's your mother, and Diana?"

"Are you hurt? You're all right? Come into the library, there's a fire there. Oh, Michael, you're here, and safe."

"Of course I am." He kissed her again, smiling slightly, and repeated, "Where's Diana?"

"Michael?" Lady Rushden hurried down the stairs. "Where's Roger?"

Michael's head hung. "I don't know."

"Let him sit down, Mama, where it's warm," Anne said firmly, and soon they had ushered him in by the fire. Anne glanced at Calvert, who nodded, and just that simply a meal was ordered. She arranged Michael in a chair drawn up to the blaze, sat on a footstool at his knee, and took one of his cold hands between her own.

"I stayed as long as I could. Nobody could find him. There wasn't a trace." Exhaustion dragged down the corners of his mouth.

"We'll talk later, my love," Anne soothed. "Here's Calvert with something for you to eat. Please, Michael."

"If it makes you happy." He looked uninterestedly at the plate of ham and trimmings set on a low table before him. "Where's Diana?"

"Here." She no longer carried the cane, but still limped a little as she moved into the room. "No news of Roger, I take it? Trust him to take his own sweet time about returning." She seated herself casually. "Try the sauce, Michael, it's really quite good. Caro and I devised it this morning."

Anne saw her betrothed's eyes widen and begin to spark with anger. Quickly she said, "Diana's right; you must eat." She spread a napkin over his knees.

"I'm quite eager to hear about the battle," Diana went on, unperturbed. "And we've had some excitement here, as well, you know. Elizabeth and Lord Gerald are married now. I'm afraid your mother and sister are declining to address us here at Midfield. You and Anne will have to charm them into coming to your wedding. We can't have one family not speaking to the other, you know. I'm sure Roger will be vastly unamused, but it serves him right for not coming home in time to settle things." She went on talking in her usual way, sharing news as Michael ate and the other two ladies sat in miserable silence. Finally Diana rose and excused herself, limping from the room. Lady Rushden gazed after her for a moment, then said something about having Michael's room prepared for him, and left.

"That's enough," Michael said, pushing the little table away. Then after a moment he burst out, "What ails Diana? You'd think I'd come in from the hunt after having lost the fox, rather than—"

"I don't know," Anne replied dejectedly. "She doesn't talk to me, except as you heard just now. She's been very strange."

He got up and began to pace, his movements made abrupt and jerky by nervous fatigue. "I didn't want to come home. Wellesley commanded me. I rode over every inch of ground I could, and I couldn't find Roger. We found the Frenchman, though, dead under a pile of leaves. In the forest, on the road we'd been taking. All the while I kept thinking, my God, what effect will all this have on Diana? I thought she'd grown to care about him, you see. And now I come home to find this!''

"Michael, dearest." Anne rose and took his hands. "Come, darling, you'll make yourself ill.''

"I couldn't find him! He might be dead, and she—''

"Michael!''

"Perhaps she feels herself happily released from an unwanted connexion," he said bitterly.

"She loves Roger! She does!''

Michael looked down at her, his brows lifting skeptically. "Does she?'' he asked pointedly, and Anne had no answer.

He slept the clock round. The servants walked on tiptoe past his room, and the whole house was hushed. No one expected him to come down to dinner, let alone done up in full evening dress, as was the custom at Midfield even among the family. Diana welcomed him prettily, had many amusing things to say about the elopement and its consequences, and made several offhand remarks about Roger's scandalous tardiness in coming home, which she attributed variously to the lure of dark and lovely Portuguese eyes, the charm of the country itself, and the joys of an incognito tour. Anne watched Michael's looks become ever blacker as he greeted with glacial silence every witticism Diana heaped upon Roger's absent head. She was magnificent in diamonds and satin, with Roger's great emerald-and-diamond ring weighing her finger down as always. She did twist it now and then in what might have been taken for nerves if her conversation had not been so perfectly calm.

"She is heartless, absolutely heartless," Michael raged in private to Anne later that night. "Roger could be dead, and I swear she'd laugh on his grave!''

"You do her an injustice, Michael," Anne replied uncomfortably.

"Do I? Never mind. When Roger gets back, he'll know how to deal with her. I can hardly wait!''

It might have comforted the minds of both if they could have seen Diana in her room that very moment. In one hand she held

Roger's cold, formal little note of farewell, and in the other was crushed the chart of his family genealogy drawn for her months before. Trickling slowly down her face were bitter tears.

The object of all this worry and suffering was at that very instant taking his ease in a huge iron bathtub in British Headquarters at Lisbon. With a cigar in one hand and a glass of French brandy from Marshal Junot's own bottles in the other, Roger lazed in blissful abandon, submerged in hot, scented water to his collarbones. Below, the generals and diplomats were dithering away, as generals and diplomats were wont to do. Their voices reached him very faintly, and he pulled a wry face. But he concentrated on listening to the melancholy strains of a guitar being played in the courtyard outside his window. The gypsy melody reminded him of the last time he had seen Diana. She had been in her green velvet, coin necklace and veil for Anne's ball, scandalously barefoot, and thoroughly beautiful. But the picture of her he conjured through the steam of his bath showed her wearing somewhat less.

Not all the weeks of his absence had been spent in so congenial a fashion or in so hospitable a place as this luxurious room. He had killed the French officer after a duel in the forest with swords and fists, then fortified himself against the chill of oncoming darkness with the contents of the man's wineskin and his uniform coat. He had not reckoned on his own weakness, which had brought on several fainting spells as he buried the Frenchman under a pile of leaves, and he had been forced to curl up under a tree to wait for the warmth of morning and the lessening of the pain in his thigh.

A patriotic Portuguese had discovered him, knocked him on the head, and thrown him across the saddle of a sturdy packhorse for a tortuously long ride to a small villa high in the hills. Fever brought on by his leg wound had kept him from consciousness for longer than he could accurately estimate, but when he had finally woken—clearheaded, if shaky—it was to the highly distressing discovery that the coat had caused his captors to think him a French spy. The torrent of Portuguese raging above his head as he pretended unconsciousness apprised him of this fact, as well as the even more distressful information that as soon as he was well enough to stand, he would be propped up against the pink walls of the villa and shot.

Protestations had gotten him exactly nowhere. He had used his sketchy but adequate Portuguese to explain that he was English, but the gnarled old crone who nursed him naturally assumed he was lying to save his life. Roger would gladly have recited what he knew of the Magna Carta and sung "God Save the King" if he had thought it would have done any good, but provincial stubbornness and patriotic pride at having caught a hated French invader were too formidable. Frustrated and increasingly alarmed, he tried to point out that the French coat did not even fit him, being too short in the arms and too snug across the shoulders, but the finer sartorial points were beyond the crone's understanding.

Hoarding his strength while pretending weakness, Roger had finally seized upon opportunity and slipped out of the bed, tottering his way to the small balcony to which he had been taken a few times to get some sun. An agonising drop of fifteen feet to the rough, moss-slick cobblestones had nearly robbed him of consciousness, but he bit back his groans of pain as his leg wound reopened and somehow climbed the short wall under cover of a cloudy, rain-scented night.

Walking to Lisbon dressed in a nightshirt not being Roger's idea of amusement, he had stolen some clothes at the nearest village and a horse at the next. The little animal reminded him of the Welsh mountain pony his father had given him on his fifth birthday. But a quarter of a century—not to mention many stones of weight and three feet of height—separated him from the child who had galloped across the downs at Midfield. Thus his progress, with bare feet more often than not dragging on the ground, was not swift. And as he neared the capital at last he began to suffer agonies at the notion of riding into the city in so undignified a manner. Still, he could not abandon the sturdy pony, and he owed it to the owner to return the beast.

Thus the scion of one of the oldest and proudest baronies in England arrived at British Headquarters limping ahead of a horse not even as tall as his shoulder. Barefoot, bearded, filthy, and hungry, Roger presented himself at the front door of the townhouse where Sir Hew resided, informed the footman of his name, rank, and need for a talk with Sir Hew—and barely restrained himself from planting his fist squarely in the jaw of a face convulsed with hilarity.

Roger was spared any further indignity by the happy arrival of Sir Hew from a conference. He was whisked inside and barely given time to wash his face and devour a plate of cold beef before Sir Hew reentered the sitting room with a horde of other officers to demand where the hell Roger had been for the last seven weeks.

At last, shaved and clean, with a crisp linen nightshirt and a dressing gown laid out on the bed, with a full meal inside him and the glow of Cognac spreading rapidly through his body, Roger relaxed and gave a great sigh as he listened to the melancholy music of the guitar. The bath water had cooled, but he lingered awhile to luxuriate. Seven weeks, he mused. His family must be frantic. Sir Hew had told him of Michael's search and offered to send word at once to Midfield apprising them of his safety. But Roger had declined this, saying that he would just as soon appear himself, in person, to reassure his mother and sisters. About Diana, his feelings were rather more complicated.

Not that he had any doubt that he cared deeply for her. He intended to have her, if only for a few months, or a few weeks, or a few days; he intended to take her to wife. He had no delusions about his lucky escape from death in Portugal, and he knew that between now and January something would happen to kill him, according to family tradition. But nobility of sentiment and largesse of soul be damned—he wanted her. She was very young; a year's mourning for him, and she'd doubtless marry again brilliantly and be happy with her next husband. Their own time together must necessarily be brief, but Roger wanted her. After his death, she could find another peer, who could have her with Roger's goodwill.

Well, not precisely his goodwill. Having been the centre of seven women's existence for most of his life, he balked at the thought of his widow finding a replacement for him. The idea of his Diana in another man's arms—

But was she his? And this was the crux of his problems. On the one hand, he could still see her throwing his ring to the floor and hear her virulent abuse. But on the other, he could also still hear her shouting that he was hers and would stay so until she said otherwise. The outrageous teasing that indicated her interest also demonstrated her indifference; her kisses were sweet memories and yet reassured him of exactly nothing.

Two days later he was deep in the throes of seasickness again. The British frigate upon which he sailed was considerably stouter and much less leaky than the little ship that had taken him to Portugal, but the effect of even the calmest seas on his stomach and equilibrium was appalling. Sunk in misery, he stayed in his cabin and groaned all the way to Portsmouth, reflecting not upon love, desire, and Diana, but upon his own agonies.

# =18=

DIANA RECLINED EXHAUSTEDLY on the green velvet cushions in her bedroom at Midfield, telling herself she had earned her rest. It had become no easier in the last weeks to pretend to Roger's mother and sisters and Michael that Roger was safe and sound; the strain showed in her dark-circled eyes and hollowed cheeks.

It was raining, and she determinedly focused her mind on the wind-driven storm sounds as she eased her feet up onto the chaise. The thing was a marvel of moss-green velvet and dark wood, and made her feel as if she should be floating down the Nile in it rather than sitting in an English country house. Closing her eyes, she tried to imagine herself drifting along palm-covered banks. But as ever, the vision that came to her was of Roger. The superstitious dread in her heart took up its sick, heavy pounding again, echoing in time to the rain on the roof, and she shivered.

There were no distractions to be had today. Lady Rushden was paying her usual Sunday afternoon visit to the vicar, and the twins were with her. Michael and Anne were at Chetley Castle for a few days. Diana was alone in the house, but for the servants and her own fears.

The previous night she had gone to dine at a local squire's, playing once again her part of unconcern. She was well aware that her facade had kept up Lady Rushden's spirits and prevented the twins from succumbing to despair. But Anne wore a cold, sad expression these days, and Michael was barely polite to her. These things hurt, yet she knew she could not weaken. Even though she believed in her heart that Roger was lost forever, she would not allow herself outward shows of grief. The effect of her performance on Lady Rushden was too important; Diana knew that she and only she was the glue that held Midfield together. By her example life went on in its regular pattern. Callers came and went, invitations were given and accepted, and when anyone mentioned Roger's name, Diana quickly forestalled incipient fears by making some laughing remark. Surely, she reasoned, this was best for everyone. Until they knew for certain, there was no reason to give way to distress. It was better for all concerned that they go on as always, and in their hearts prepared themselves for the loss. Diana held herself in check constantly—a new experience for her—and suffered in private, alone.

"My lady! My lady!"

Her maid's voice, raised louder than usual beyond the door of the room, roused her. "Come in." She sat up, composing herself.

"My lady—downstairs—" The girl gulped.

Diana groaned softly. What a miserable time to come calling, was her first thought; her second, as she went to the mirror to rub some colour into her pale cheeks, how lucky that someone is come, so that I need not sit alone. "I'll be down directly. Who is it?"

"I—I did not catch his name, my lady."

Her brows arched. "Very well. Tell whoever it is to wait for me in the drawing room."

"Very good, my lady."

Diana curved her lips into a smile as she descended the stairs, wondering who her caller might be. She twisted the immense ring on her finger, a nervous gesture she had developed over the last months, then consciously relaxed her hands. At the door of the drawing room a terrible idea slammed into her and she swayed. Perhaps the caller was from the War Office and would tell her that Roger's body had been found. Her heart set up its thick pounding again, the carvings of the door misting dizzily before her eyes. Then, with the stern control she had been practising, she steadied herself to face the worst. Nodding to the footman, who opened the door for her, she stepped into the room with her face, if not her mind, calm.

"Well, Diana?"

Her thoughts darted like birds. Such was her confusion that she could neither move nor speak, only stare at the tall, rawboned man with sun-bleached hair who stood near the fire. His skin was darkly browned, his eyes the more brilliant in contrast. Where was the casual elegance, the sardonic glance, the curl of his lips that meant he was about to make some acid remark at her expense?

"Have you no tender words of welcome for the returned traveller?"

His voice was the same, clear and soft. With a supreme effort she walked a few paces forward and smiled faintly. "Do you make a long stay in England, my lord?" she asked coolly, with joy, anger, relief, and insult battling each other to a standstill in her heart. She would not gratify his conceit; he would have no cause to laugh at her. He was home and safe; he was so thin; he had not even smiled at her. "I wonder you forsook the sunshine of Portugal for all this rain."

A little muscle jumped in his cheek and he went very pale beneath his tan. But his wide mouth curved in the old way as he made her a mocking bow. "To return was always my primary object. For who could wish to forego so warm a welcome home? I note that I need not have had any anxieties for what you might have suffered on my behalf. You appear more unmoved than even I myself to find me alive."

Diana bit back the hot retort that rose to her lips. How dared he use her thus when she had nearly died of fear for him? "You must regale me with the full tale of your adventures, my lord, at the earliest opportunity. Did you find Portugal pleasant?"

"I recommend it most heartily. Won't you sit down?"

She advanced a few more steps, blanching as he limped to a chair and seated himself without waiting for her. "You were wounded?" she faltered.

"Nothing to signify."

"Trust the devil to look after his own," she snapped.

"I believe you have hit on the very reason why I am not mouldering in some hillside ditch, rather than enjoying your charming company," Roger remarked casually.

"That is just like you!" Diana flared. "Wondering why you're not dead instead of rejoicing that you're alive!"

"And is there a reason for me to rejoice, my dear Lady Diana?" he shot back at once. "I seem to have deprived you of your chance to play the bereaved bride—a role that would have suited you much better than that of my wife. However," he continued lazily, his lids drooping over his bright, sharp eyes, "it would appear that neither of us has a choice. Only name the day, my dear, and after that you may practise your widow's wails. I must say, you'll look perfectly ravishing in black."

Quivering with rage and hurt, she was about to strip off his ring again and this time throw it in his face. All her old dramatic impulsiveness returned in a rush. But in the instant her fingers touched the heavy stone, the drawing room doors parted and Lady Rushden ran in with the twins. With shrieks of delight they welcomed their returned hero in a shower of tears and kisses. Diana left the room and went upstairs to pack.

The next morning she remained in her room, writing her note to Lady Rushden explaining her abrupt and unannounced departure, for she had told no one that she was leaving and intended to accomplish a Napoleonic fait accompli. She had spent the whole night folding and packing her gowns with vicious speed. But at barely ten in the morning a commotion outside her window heralded an unexpected and wholly amazing development: the duchess of Sturbrough had arrived.

Her Grace had not left the immediate environs of London in twenty years. Thus her sudden appearance at Midfield mystified everyone, especially as enough boxes and trunks were unloaded from her carriage to indicate an ominously long stay. Diana was called down to greet the duchess and within the quarter-hour found herself seated in the library alone with that formidable lady. The rest of the family had been summarily dismissed.

"So," Her Grace said. "You and that idiot nephew of mine have not yet reached an understanding."

"Whatever can Your Grace mean?" Diana responded icily.

"Don't be impertinent with me, girl. Are you engaged or not?"

"We are." She got to her feet. "Will that be all?"

"Not by a long chalk. Sit down."

"I beg Your Grace to excuse me. I have my packing to attend to."

"Packing? Running away? I never took you for a coward! Fool, yes, but not a coward!"

Stung, Diana sat.

"There. That's more like it. Now, are you going to allow Roger to fiddle about like the imbecile he is, or are you going to make this charade of a betrothal into the real thing?"

Diana leapt to her feet again. "I have not the slightest intention of running after him like a lovesick ninny!" she snapped. "If you thought I would do so, you have been sadly mistaken in my character. May I have Your Grace's leave to withdraw?"

"No. Sit down."

Diana's patience snapped. "No!" She glared down at the old woman.

The duchess glared right back, then began to laugh. "Oh, how you remind me of myself at your age! Give as good as you get, and the devil with anyone who pricks at your pride, eh? Now that we understand each other, let us speak more sensibly. And do sit down, my dear. You give me a crick in my neck, with your jumping up and down like a jack-in-the-box."

Diana glowered. The duchess lifted her elegant eyebrows. Diana hesitated. The duchess pointed a bejewelled finger at a chair. And Diana, with poor grace, sat down.

"Now. Since Anne and that lackwit Michael will be married from here—"

"In London," Diana corrected.

"I think not. The earl will be perfectly content to avoid a long hobble down the aisle of St. Paul's. They'll be married here, in early January—the third, I think. Yes." The duchess smiled like a cat one instant away from a successful pounce. "The third will do very nicely. Do you think that between now and then you can work Roger around? God knows how you managed it last spring, when this whole silly business was concocted."

Diana met the duchess's bright, challenging eyes. A reluctant smile began on her face. "I might," she allowed.

"I thought as much. The Rushden men have never had an iota of sense when it comes to their women. When Roger's father was pursuing my sister Georgiana—well, that's another tale, too long for the telling. But depend upon it, child, Roger will attempt all sorts of nonsense to trap you without admitting that he's in love with you. If you're clever, you'll end by trapping him." The duchess chuckled. "Just as he deserves. Someday you'll have to tell me precisely how you got him to agree to be your fiancé in the first place."

Diana's lips twitched. Then she grinned at the duchess. "Would you like to hear it now?"

"You've unpacking to do," the duchess pointed out.

Diana gave a start. How could she have been so foolish as to even think of leaving? She gabbled an apology to the duchess and raced out of the library.

Anne joined her shortly before teatime, when the last of her things were being replaced in their drawers. Michael had commandeered the two swiftest horses in his father's stables, and he and Anne had ridden at all speed for Midfield upon receipt of Lady Rushden's note that Roger was home. Her cheeks were still pink with the tears she had wept over her brother as Diana welcomed her in and shut the door. Hiding her grin as Anne visibly steeled herself for the encounter, Diana went on folding her nightdresses.

"I came to ask if everything is all right," Anne said, taking in the import of the portmanteaux.

"I've been unpacking. Don't ask, Annie. I've seen the error of my ways, I assure you, and am staying for your wedding."

Anne's face was a study in bewilderment. "But—how did you know? We only decided yesterday to move the site from London to the church here!"

Diana giggled. "I have my sources. And it will be a wonderful wedding."

"Will it?" Anne asked pointedly. "Roger is to walk me down the aisle, and you're to be my chief attendant. It would look very odd if you're not speaking to each other!"

Diana gave her friend a sidelong glance and pushed a drawer shut. "I shouldn't worry about that."

"Di!" Anne paced, then rounded on her. "I'll have no evasions from you. Do you intend to marry him?"

"Of course. Whatever gave you the idea that I didn't?"

"You've been—oh, Diana, you've been perfectly beastly and you know it!"

Contrite now, Diana went to her friend and took her slim hands. "Forgive me. I know how it must have seemed to you."

"Do you love him? Really?"

"If you doubt my intentions, only have a look at this." She went to the little desk and took out a small velvet box. Handing it to Anne with a smile, she asked, "Well? Am I serious?"

"Oh!" The lid opened to reveal a signet ring. "He said he'd lost his in Portugal, but—it's beautiful, but it's scarcely a wedding ring!"

"Look again," Diana advised.

Anne did so, her brow clouding. "These are not the Rushden arms."

"Indeed they are not. My cousin Charles negotiated a perfectly vicious contract, you know. There's a clause in it that quarters the Bellrose arms with yours. I am my father's heiress and the last of my name, you know." She giggled once again. "Your lion's head and my roses. It's rather pretty, isn't it? Do you think Roger will notice?"

Anne gaped at her before bursting into relieved laughter. "Di, you're impossible! How did you get him to agree? Our arms have never been quartered with anyone's, despite the heiresses our men have married."

"None of the other heiresses had a Cousin Charles. He's very clever. And besides, Roger is so convinced that the marriage will never take place that he probably signed without having read."

"I wanted to talk to you about that," Anne said, closing the box and setting it aside. "How will you convince him? He's still deluding himself about that silly curse, and—"

"And that's why he signed without reading. Think how furious he'll be when he has to live up to the letter of the contract!" Diana crowed.

"Diana! How are you going to make him go through with it?"

"Several notions had occurred to me," she replied airily. "One or two of them not entirely respectable. Oh, don't look at me that way. Those would be my last resort. But trust the devil to look after his own," she quoted herself. "Besides, how should an engagement that began with false pretenses and trickery end but with more deception? Once we are married, it will be time enough to resort to the dullness of honesty."

"My poor brother," Anne said with a sigh, shaking her head. "Has he any idea of the wife he's getting in you?"

"I trust so," Diana purred.

# —19—

ROGER SAW MUCH of what he would be getting over the next weeks, although he felt again as he had in the spring. Everyone conspired against him to prevent his having an instant alone with Diana. Michael's attitude underwent a marked shift, and from his initial icy politeness, which puzzled Roger greatly, he reverted to his old playful teasing of Diana. As November and December wore on, however, Michael began to glower and fidget, his temper wearing thin as his nuptials approached. Roger displayed similar symptoms, and from not entirely dissimilar causes.

One event alone distracted the whole party, and this came on the day after Christmas. A Royal equerry arrived with an elaborately crested and sealed document that disclosed that because of the Rushden family's long and distinguished service to the Crown, and especially because of the current baron's actions in Portugal, which had contributed to the victory there, His Majesty's Government was pleased to act upon recommendations and hereby informed the twenty-eighth baron that henceforth he would be the first viscount. Roger's only publicly expressed reaction was to wonder how loudly HRH had howled when persuaded to countenance the honour.

Lady Rushden's observation was that although it was high time the family was formally recognised, it had always been a point of pride with them that their barony was one of the oldest in England. So many dukes, marquesses, and earls had been created for doubtful motives—King Charles the Second's elevation of his mistresses and bastard children, for instance—that the ancient barons clung to their less exalted but more traditionally earned titles.

The duchess announced her opinion that "certain persons" had taken long enough in following her suggestion, and then turned to Diana to enquire how she would enjoy being a viscountess.

"Oh, the same as Annie will, I expect," Michael replied for her, sliding an arm around his lady's waist. "Only another week, my love!"

"And Caroline's dress not yet finished!" the duchess reminded them all. "You have work yet to do."

"My work has not yet begun—unfortunately," Michael said with a sigh.

"Cawker!" The duchess's abuse was always in direct proportion to her fondness for its object, and since she had always been fond of both the earl and Michael, her abuse of both was almost constant. "Go on, Anne, and you too, Diana. Leave Roger to his title, and this lackwit to his frustrations."

The younger ladies grinned and swept out of the room, and that was the end of the discussion of Roger's new styles and dignities. There was, to all minds, more important business to hand.

The guests began to arrive on the morning of the first day of the new year of 1809. Because it was winter, the guest list was rather smaller than it might have been and everyone could be accommodated at Midfield itself. By nightfall the drawing rooms, small salons, hallways, and even the dining room were packed with people, driving the servants to distraction as they attempted to go about their duties. Roger, as head of the house, supervised the arrangements for his guests' entertainment, which on the morning of the second included a hunt.

Of course he had a plan for encountering Diana alone, although his avowed intention was to secure a deer for the wedding feast. His mother and aunt snorted at this; Midfield was provisioned with enough to feed the Peninsular Army. But it was Roger's happy design that one of his presents to the bridal pair would be the horns of a magnificent stag, and to this end the ladies and gentlemen brave enough to face the numbing snows bundled into their hunting clothes and onto their mounts.

Diana, up on a fleet Arab mare and extremely fetching in a bottle-green habit, took the opportunity to forget her frustrating attempts to encounter Roger alone and force him into a declaration. The conspiracy, she had realised in the last few days, enveloped her, too. She strongly suspected that it was the duchess's doing, in collusion with Anne and Michael and even the twins. All her elaborate plans for coming upon Roger alone, and her prepared speeches to ensnare him, were for nothing. But with the wind tearing at her hat and hair as her grey Arab sailed over ditches and fences, she regained her natural optimism. If the duchess had planned their separation, she might also have planned a suitable dénouement. Diana trusted Her Grace implicitly. Thus she could set her mind at rest and spend a lovely morning galloping wildly across the hills, not really caring whether she was following the hunt.

This was precisely what Roger had wanted. The pale colour of Diana's mare's coat made its rider easy to spot, and when the hunt went in one direction over the downs towards the woods, and Diana rode to one side, Roger grinned and followed her.

He caught her up at the river, where she had slowed to walk her tired horse and try to pin up her cascading hair. "Your name suits you ill, madam," he called, and had the satisfaction of watching all the pins fall from her hair as her hands dropped to the reins and she turned her head quickly. "Diana was the huntress, and you've lost the stag completely."

"Killing helpless animals is not my idea of sport," she returned tartly, attempting in vain to coil her hair around itself without the convenience of pins. The mare sidestepped a little as Roger's huge sorrel stallion approached, and she maintained her balance in the sidesaddle with difficulty.

"Allow me." Roger grinned. He took her reins and enjoyed the flash of her eyes.

"I'm perfectly capable—" she began.

"How dull! Perfectly capable women are so boring. I would rather have you perfectly incapable." He swung off his horse, tied his reins and Diana's to a bush, and summarily seized her around the waist. Lifting her to the ground, he retained his hold on her and laughed down at her outraged protests. "Incapable of speech, that is," he added, and kissed her firmly on the mouth.

Lady Diana slapped his face. Lord Rushden laughed and kissed her again. Her nails raked down his cheek. He stopped laughing, took both her wrists in a bruising grip, and pinned them behind her back. As his lips touched hers again she suddenly went sweetly pliant in his arms—and bit him.

The haste with which Roger released her caused Diana to lose her balance. Stumbling back from him, her breath coming in panting gasps not entirely due to outrage, she lost her footing and landed in a bush. Roger, one hand to his sore lower lip, burst out laughing again.

"Oh, God!" he cried between paroxysms, "you are the damnedest woman!"

"Damn *you*!" she shouted back, floundering helplessly as her dress, hat, and veil caught on various branches and rendered her incapable of rising. It was inelegant to rage at a man from so undignified a position, and she thrashed about furiously, tearing her habit and working herself ever deeper into the tangles of the bush. "Don't just stand there, you idiot! Get me out of here!"

"I rather think I like you there." He grinned insolently. "Since you'll have to listen to me, will you, nill you."

"Roger! Help me up!"

"Only if you'll promise to elope with me," he teased.

"Elope!" She succeeded in tearing her hat and veil off her head entirely and, freed of its encumberment, sat up. She tugged at her habit, aware suddenly that quite a bit of booted leg and not a little stockinged thigh were presented to his interested view. "Never!"

"Come now, you felt no compunction about assisting Lizzie and Lord Gerald," he said, folding his arms and regarding her as if she sat on a velvet sopha rather than in a hawthorne bush. "Surely I have demonstrated that my passion for you is quite equal to his for her. Does that not constitute an admirable excuse for an elopement?"

Diana gaped at him, forgetting the display of her legs and her ridiculous position. "How—how did you learn of that?"

"My dear sister regaled me with the whole tale several days ago, after their arrival for the wedding. Most instructive. Scandalous of you, certainly, but it indicated to me that your pretty notions of a long engagement and a formal marriage amidst friends and relations could be overcome. Come, Diana, let's escape together. I promise I will not be above, oh, two or three weeks in getting the special licence required, and think what fun we could have in the meantime!"

"Oh!" she cried inadequately. "*Oh!* You—you *beast!* You rotten, miserable, insulting, indecent, immoral, horrible—"

"Beast?" he finished for her as she ran out of invective. Grinning, he held out a hand to help her to her feet. It was ignored, and he watched in high amusement as she struggled to rise. Her habit ripped in several places before she had staggered upright, and her first action was to march over to him and strike him full in the face.

"I hate you!" she shrieked. "You are loathsome! From the very first you've done nothing but insult me! I wish to God you *had* been killed in Portugal!" And with that she gathered her bedraggled skirts, clambered up on her mare, and rode off.

Roger's emotions had undergone a complete and profound reversal during her speech. He stared after her, all amusement gone, the wound she had inflicted resolving into an ache that rent his heart. He had gone too far, played too blithely with her easily ignited temper, and the truth that was his reward pierced his very soul.

He climbed wearily back onto his horse and rode slowly back to Midfield, where that night he and Michael fulfilled tradition and got very drunk.

# ═20═

THE DAWN WAS crystalline in its beauty, diamond drops hanging from every tree and bush so that it seemed Midfield had bedecked itself in jewels to celebrate the wedding of its favourite daughter. The bridegroom was rousted out of his bed at seven, after a mere four hours' sodden sleep, and roared his outrage so loudly that the duchess sent her maid to enquire of Lady Rushden if she had taken to housing wild animals. The entire wing of the house was awakened, and the earl's suggestion for the containment of his son met with Roger's wholehearted approval. Several of the young men were enlisted and Michael was carried, howling, downstairs to be deposited on the snowy lawns in his dressing gown. The application of a flurry of snowballs cleared his head enough to turn the skirmish into a full-scale war, and only Lady Rushden's frantic protests stopped them all in time to prevent multiple cases of pneumonia.

"What in the name of God do you think you were doing?" her ladyship scolded as she instructed his man to help her only son out of his soaked clothes and into a hot bath. "Are you trying to kill yourself?"

Roger shot her a dark look she did not understand, then smiled and waved a hand. "No, Mama," he replied obediently. "Just trying to wake Michael. He has to be able to say the right thing when he marries Annie today, you know. Dreadful scandal if he fell asleep at the altar."

Twelve hours later Lady Rushden surveyed the ruins of the wedding luncheon. Not a single guest had gotten up from it, so perforce it had been turned into a wedding dinner as well, whose most spectacular feature was the roast stag brought out on an immense platter by three sweating servants and greeted with roars of laughter. Calvert, fidgeted nearly witless by the disinclination of the guests to leave the dining room, consulted with her ladyship and then approached his lordship.

"It's getting on for eight o'clock, my lord," he began reasonably. "The viscount might wish to begin thinking about his departure."

Wide blue eyes blinked owlishly. "Departure? Where am I going, Calvert?"

"Not you, my lord. The other viscount. Lord Hulme. He and Miss Anne, or rather her ladyship the viscountess—"

"Michael!" His lordship leaned across the table and bellowed, "Are you trying to abduct my sister again?"

"They're married now," Diana informed him coldly. "It is perfectly proper for them to leave together."

"Leave?" he asked plaintively. "Don't they like the party?"

"My lord," Calvert tried again, "it is a four-hour drive to Boyden Lodge."

"Couldn't say," was the airy response. "Never been there."

Calvert exchanged a speaking look with Lady Diana and wisely withdrew.

She had been cursing herself ever since her temper had cooled the previous evening. It had been grossly cruel of her to say what she had said to Roger, and she had promised herself to apologise no matter how much it cost her pride. But no opportunity had presented itself, the conspiracy to keep them apart being unnecessary in the bustle of the wedding. Her shame had held her silent all day, her behaviour so glacial that she had intercepted several worried glances from Anne. But in the face of Roger's absurdly endearing drunkenness, Diana felt her constraint melting away. Leaning around Lady Rushden's back, she tugged at Anne's sleeve. "You'll never get there at this rate, Anne. What do you say to another snowball fight?"

Anne regarded her wedded lord with a skeptical eye and shook her head. "A blizzard wouldn't sober him." She winced as Roger and Michael began to sing a scandalous regimental drinking song.

"Two blizzards," she amended.

"Roger!" Diana shook his arm. He stopped singing and glared at her. "Roger, we must see Anne and Michael on their way now."

The glower was replaced by a sunny smile. "Splendid idea. And so to bed, eh?" Getting to his feet, he roared out, "Michael! To horse!"

Michael was on his feet instantly, looking for his sword. It had been removed from his belt and immediate vicinity by his father, who had wisely judged the effects of alcohol and happiness on his son's already delicate condition, and had taken all sharp objects from his reach. Bewildered, Michael searched his belt, then paused and wailed, "But Roger, I am only just married! You cannot be so cruel!"

"Out!" Roger cried, weaving slightly. Diana steadied him with a hand at the small of his back. "Out of my house! Take the wench across your saddle if you must, but ride out of here!" He stumbled, landed back in his chair, and beamed at Diana. "See? I did it," he said proudly.

"Oh, God!" Anne moaned. "Diana, do something with him!"

"Splendid idea!" Roger grinned again. Then a tragic look came into his eyes, his face assuming sorrowful lines. "But Diana's not even speaking to me. She wouldn't elope with me, she doesn't love me, she is not talking to me."

"Only to tell you to be still," Diana assured him.

"I'm sorry about the bush," he mumbled. Then, sinking down into his chair with a long sigh, his eyes drooped closed.

"You are disgustingly drunk, both of you," Anne said.

"I quite agree," came the duchess's glacial tones. "Reginald," she said to the earl, "take your miserable son outside and soak his head in the nearest horse trough. You may use my nephew's head to break through any ice. Anne, Diana, attend me." She rose majestically to her feet. "Georgiana," she directed at her sister, "I leave the arrangement of your guests up to you. But I shall expect everyone to be outside and ready to bid farewell to this ill-assorted couple within the quarter-hour."

The iron authority of the duchess, plus the cooperation of Michael's father and Anne's mother, produced the required miracle. Less serious measures than a dousing in frigid water procured a degree of sobriety in Roger and Michael; Anne was dressed in her travelling costume in record time; and Calvert, closing the doors of the dining room at last, breathed a sigh of relief and blessed the duchess before directing the footmen and maids to get busy putting the room in order.

Diana kissed and embraced Anne, then stood back while Lady Rushden and Anne's five sisters did the same. Roger gave Michael a hearty slap on the shoulder that nearly felled him, and swept Anne into his arms.

"Can't think of a better way to show you both I love you than to give you to him as his wife," he told her.

"Wait a few months into the marriage," was the earl's prediction with a wicked gleam in his eyes. "Then ask them if they thank you for this day's work!"

"It isn't the day's, but the night's that concerns me!" Michael, the irrepressible, chortled. He bent over Diana's hand, collected his prize, and then they were gone, clattering down the drive on their way to Boyden Lodge.

"Well," said Lady Rushden with a sigh. "That's done with. My nerves are quite shredded. Still, all the ladies cried and it went off very well." She cast a reproachful eye at Lady Gerald. "You see what you missed out on, madam!"

"Mama," Elizabeth pleaded.

"Georgiana, go to bed," ordered the duchess. "All these people are waiting for your example."

"Margaret," her sister replied with some annoyance, "have you considered that not only is this my home, but that some of my guests might wish some supper?"

"You had best rethink your ownership, my dear," was the scathing retort, with a significant glance at Diana that mortified the girl. "And as for food—they've been eating all day. Go to bed, all of you! Shoo!" Then, commandingly, "Not you, Diana."

Her Grace's glare dispersed the guests. Diana lingered as requested, her eyes on Roger as he climbed the stairs with Elizabeth and Lord Gerald. Drunk as he was, he retained his grace of movement and was as elegant as if he had just stepped from his valet's ministrations.

"Calvert, I tasted some goodish Madeira the other night. Would you do me the favour of bringing some to the library?"

"At once, Your Grace."

"Always treat your servants with more respect than you do your family," the duchess advised Diana as they walked down the hall. "It does wonders for the morale of both. Now," she continued, seating herself in an armchair drawn up before the blazing fire. "Tell me your wedding plans."

"I doubt if there will be a wedding," Diana said morosely as she sat down. "I've been a fool."

"Granted, but, then, so is Roger. You're well matched. He's looking very ragged around the edges, you know—a most encouraging sign."

Calvert entered with a tray of wine and biscuits, stayed long enough to pour, and left. The duchess brought out a pack of cards and Diana set up a table between them. She expected the game to provide employment while they discussed Roger, but instead the duchess talked about everything but her nephew. And before Diana knew it, the clock in the hall had chimed half past eleven.

"No, don't leave me yet," the duchess said, reshuffling the cards. "I'm not yet sleepy enough for bed."

Diana poured another measure of wine into their glasses. "I'll miss Michael and Anne."

"Yes. She suits him. But, more important, he suits her. It's always best when the woman is more contented in her choice than the man is. Women understand happiness, you see. By making her own, she ensures her husband's as well."

"That sounds rather selfish."

"Of course! I've never held with the notion of noble sacrifice. Absurd idea. Produces nothing but resentment and guilt."

Diana reflected on the resentment and guilt that her own selfishness had brought her, and was about to make a comment to that effect when she realised the lovely old eyes were fixed on the mantelpiece clock. The duchess noted Diana's curious look, and dealt out the cards again. But as they played, her eyes kept straying to the slowly moving hands of the gilt timepiece. The cards were set aside. Diana began to shift nervously in her chair as the old lady's tension began to affect her. Shadows gathered around them as the candles in their tall silver branches sputtered and died. The fire in the hearth burnt itself down to thin flames and then smouldering coals. Held silent, almost enthralled, Diana did not even move to chafe her chilled fingers. The duchess kept staring at the clock, and the minute hand crept toward twelve.

At last the hall chimes rang softly and the clock on the mantel clasped its hands. The duchess sank back into her chair with a long sigh. "It is past midnight of the third," she murmured. "And Roger was thirty years old yesterday."

Diana's breath caught. "Yesterday?"

"Why do you think I insisted on the third as the date of the wedding? Thanks be to God I was the only one who remembered, with all the fuss over Michael and Anne." She smiled, an expression softer and more luminous than Diana had ever seen from her. "Go to him, child."

Diana required no further urging. She flew up the stairs, pausing in her room only long enough to retrieve the velvet box, and skimmed down the hallway to Roger's chamber. Her heart racing, she opened the door and stole silently inside.

He was sitting before the remains of the bedroom fire, moonlight through the open curtains touching his hair with silver. On the floor beside him was a nearly empty bottle of brandy, and in his hand was a nearly empty glass.

"Get out," he said.

"Roger—"

He didn't even look at her. "I said, get out. I don't want you here."

Diana took several steps into the room. "But I have something for you."

"Something to be buried with me, I trust?" He took a long pull at the brandy. "How terribly romantic of you, my dear."

"Don't be an idiot!" She bit back the rest of an angry outburst and went to his side. "It's the fourth, Roger. You're safe."

"Oh, I expect to be felled within the next ten minutes or so," he replied breezily. "How kind of you to join me in my last moments."

The sudden spill of the brandy down his shirt front as he tossed back the remains of the glass informed her that he was *very* drunk. She took the goblet from his fingers and retained her hold on his hand. Slipping the ring onto it, she released him and sat down in the chair beside his.

"What in hell is this?" He squinted at the ring.

"What does it look like?" she countered. "Really, darling, you are the most imbecile man."

The endearment had come out quite naturally, but Roger didn't seem to notice it. He was busy staring at the ring. "Good God! Of all the arrogant, ridiculous—"

"Your clock is behind time," she observed, glancing at the offending timepiece.

At last Roger looked at her. His eyes were glazed and his expression conveyed not only his confusion but his extreme state of inebriation. "What are you babbling about? What is this ring? Diana, if this is another of your torments—"

She wanted to laugh, because he really did look very funny. Comprehension slowly dawned in his face; he looked at her, then at the clock, then at her again. "My clock is behind time," he stated.

"By about a quarter-hour, I should say," she agreed.

"My God," he said quite matter-of-factly. "I'm alive."

"Of course you are. And you're very drunk as well. Why don't you go to bed now?"

Again he seemed not to have heard her. "The viscountcy," he muttered. "That must've been it. That's what broke the curse." Focusing on her again, he scowled. "What are you doing here? It's the middle of the night!"

"Merely conveying the happy news, my lord."

"Is it happy for you, Diana?"

For once in her life she could think of nothing to say. It wasn't that she had no answer for him—it was a most emphatic "yes"— but he didn't look as if that was what he wanted to hear.

"I should be furious with you," he said. "You ruined my scheme with Lady Matilda, made my life a misery, led me an intolerable dance for months. You aided and abetted my sister's elopement, infuriated me at every turn, and now you've managed to do with the Rushden arms what no other woman has ever done."

The catalogue of her offences began to anger her. Led *him* a dance? Made *his* life a misery? She opened her mouth to tell him exactly what she thought of him.

"Are you going to tell me why?"

Rebellion flickered out. "Yes, I will," she said in a subdued voice. "It was because I love you. Little as you deserve it, I do love you, Roger."

"Don't make it sound as if you didn't like it, darling," he replied. "I am convinced you will enjoy being my viscountess."

"Your viscountess?"

"Oh, really, Diana. Need I go down on one knee again? I thought we'd settled all that long ago."

He was grinning at her. She clenched her fists, got to her feet and went toward the door. "If this is your idea of a proposal—"

"It's all the proposal you're going to get, my love." He rose, swayed a little, and steadied himself by gripping the back of his chair. "Come here. I love you. Maybe I always have. And I think you've always known it. Now will you come away from that door, or shall I drag you away?"

Diana couldn't believe that a man so foxed could move so quickly, but before she knew it, she was in his arms and his lips were on hers.

"You are a torment," he murmured when finally they broke apart. "But I have a fancy to be tormented by you for the next fifty years or more."

Diana smiled. "I promise you, my lord, that I'll do my best to oblige." And she pulled his face down to hers with a deep sigh of satisfaction.

If you have enjoyed this book and would like to receive
details of other Walker Regency romances,
please write to:

Regency Editor
Walker and Company
720 Fifth Avenue
New York, N.Y. 10019